THE SHIFTING FATE SERIES

SPARK
OF FATE

TESSA HALE

Cover Design: MIBL Art
Paperback Formatting: Champagne Book Design

THE SHIFTING FATE SERIES

SPARK
OF FATE

PROLOGUE

LACEY BELTED OUT THE LYRICS TO ONE OF MY FAVORITE songs as she turned onto the two-lane road that would take us home. The sing-along would've been fun if it wasn't for the fact that she was singing in an octave that made dogs howl.

"Come on, sing with me, little sister."

"That's not singing," I yelled over the music and Lacey's screeching.

She turned down the stereo. "That's just the price you have to pay for forcing me into driving you tonight."

"I didn't *force* you."

"You looked at me with those sad puppy eyes when Mom said she was too tired."

I twisted, glancing over at Lacey. "The music wasn't that bad, was it?"

"There's a reason Jason wouldn't go with you..."

I winced at the reminder. My boyfriend had made it clear he'd rather put hot pokers in his eyes than listen to my favorite local band.

Lacey stole a quick look in my direction when I didn't say anything. "He's a tool. You know that, right? You deserve so much better, Ro."

"He's not a tool. We just don't like the same music."

"I don't like them either, but I still came with you tonight."

"And have been giving me crap the whole time."

She reached over and squeezed my leg. "Big sister prerogative."

"Big sister torture," I mumbled. Lacey loved to remind me that she was older, wiser, and a whole bunch of other things. The only thing she never used as a weapon was the fact that I was adopted. Not even during our worst fights. It was our sister code. My poor hair choices and childhood buck teeth were fair game; the fact that we weren't blood-related was not.

"Same difference." Lacey drummed her hands on the steering wheel. "You should break up with him. You know the only reason you've stayed with that douche for this long is because you're scared of the unknown."

That wasn't exactly true. But it wasn't a lie either. Jason was comfortable, easy, like a pair of slippers worn exactly the right amount. At least, that was how he had been. It felt as if things were changing. Life was moving and rearranging without my knowledge or permission. Now, nothing felt right.

"I can't imagine not being with him." Jason had been my first…everything. That was hard to walk away from.

Lacey took my hand and squeezed, the bracelets she'd bought us when we'd spent a week at the beach last summer lining up so that they were touching. "You deserve someone who accepts all the pieces that make up the beautiful human you are. Someone who lights your nerve endings on fire. Someone who'd want to go to the worst concert in the world, just for a chance to spend a little more time with you."

I eyed my sister. "And you know what that feels like?"

"Maybeeeee…" She drew the word out.

I jerked in my seat, turning to face her and pulling my hand free. "Spill. Right this second. I can't believe you've been holding out on me."

Lacey's laughter filled the car. So full and uninhibited. She never worried about what that laugh might sound like, if it was too loud or shrill or anything else. She was free. "Well, we met—"

Her words cut off as a deer darted in front of the car.

Everything went into a sort of surreal slow motion. Lacey slammed on the brakes, jerking the wheel. The light dusting of snow sent the wheels into a spin. No, not the wheels, the whole car.

The world blurred. I didn't know if Lacey was screaming or if I was. There was a sickening crunch of metal, then a shattering of glass. Pieces hit my face, slicing my skin. My side burned as if I were being stabbed with hot metal. The pain stole all the air from my lungs.

I squeezed my eyes closed, willing my breath to return, and silently crying out for anyone or anything that would listen. I gasped, the air filling my lungs again.

"Lace?" I croaked.

The only response was the hissing of our engine.

"Lacey?" I tried to turn myself to get a view of her, but I was stuck.

"Rowan?" she wheezed.

"I'm here." I stretched a hand over, finding hers. Lacey's hand was slick. Was that blood? I hooked a finger in her bracelet, as if that could keep us tethered no matter what.

My vision blurred again, and I swore I could feel my heartbeat reverberating through my whole body. "Can you reach your phone?"

"I-I don't know. It was in the cupholder."

I tried to reach my purse and cried out in pain.

Lacey sucked in a sharp breath and began to cough. Violent, racking coughs that felt as if they rocked the car.

"Are you okay? What's happening?"

She kept coughing and wheezing. It sounded wet, but I couldn't see, couldn't move. I stretched farther, trying to get to my purse. Tears streamed down my face as my side felt as if it were being ripped open.

Then everything went quiet. No more coughing. Only the hissing of the car and the blinding pain in my side.

"Lacey?" I whispered.

There was no answer.

I shook her hand. "Lace, wake up!"

Nothing.

The tears came faster, harder. I pushed my body farther, praying that I could just reach my phone. If I could get help, it would all be okay. Instead, my vision tunneled and there was nothing but black.

CHAPTER ONE

I CURLED MY KNEES UP TO MY CHEST, LEANING MY HEAD against the wall as I stared out the window. I'd wanted a window seat for as long as I could remember. A cozy little nest where I could watch the world. Now, I'd do anything to give it back. The price of the tufted cushion and pretty view were too high.

My fingers tangled in the threads of my bracelets as I stared at the rose gold beads. There were two now. Two because the owner of the other no longer walked this earth.

My heart squeezed, that same familiar pang that had punctuated so much of the past six months. Sometimes the pain came out of nowhere, as if it could sense that, just for a split second, I'd forgotten my sister was gone.

Other times, it was a steady beat in my chest, a constant reminder that because of me she'd never sing off-key while driving down country roads again. I sucked in a breath, but the air felt like it was made of razor blades.

That was the thing about grief—it made everything a million times harder. Everyone dealt with that burden differently.

My father wanted to forget. I think if my mom would've let him, he would've put every photo of Lacey into boxes in storage. He didn't have that option, so instead, he'd moved us across the country. From a suburb outside of Baltimore to the middle of nowhere Washington.

He'd traded the job he'd had for as long as I could remember at a small local accounting firm for a new one at a sleek firm in Seattle. He'd started dressing differently, got a haircut that looked like it could be found in GQ magazine instead of the same slightly shaggy one he'd had all my life. It was as if he were making himself into an entirely different person, one who hadn't had a daughter named Lacey.

I swallowed against the burn creeping up my throat. He barely remembered he had a daughter named Rowan either. We'd been here a little over a week, and his work hours kept getting longer and longer. He'd started opting to stay in a company apartment in the city during the week.

It left me to sit on the window seat alone. I didn't want to wander the house, listening to the faint strains of the television that came from his and my mom's bedroom. I didn't think she knew what graced the screen, she just needed the noise to distract her from the pain.

I shifted in my seat, letting my gaze drift away from the bracelet. The little town of Cloverdale was quaint. An hour and a half outside of Seattle, it was set at the foot of a large expanse of national forest land. Everything around us was greener than I'd ever seen before.

Dad had said it was just the place to rebuild. A place that was safe and perfect for us. Yet he wasn't here to set the foundation for whatever it was he'd envisioned.

From my window perch, I could see our picture-perfect neighborhood. I would've preferred my window to face the back of the house, where the seemingly endless forest began. That would've made me feel safe in my solitude. Protected and immune from any stares.

I watched as a couple of kids raced down the street on scooters, chased by a guy laughing as he ran. His laugh was completely uninhibited, as if not a single thing weighed on his shoulders, his head thrown back, golden-blond hair ruffling in the breeze.

His steps faltered as he passed in front of my house. He stopped in the middle of the sidewalk, and his gaze cut right to me. The deep blue of his eyes froze me to the spot. I sucked in a sharp breath, but it didn't cut like razor blades—no, this time the air felt as if it burned me from the inside out.

The guy cocked his head to one side, studying me. Something about that gaze felt like it could see everything I fought so hard to keep a lid on. All my pain and guilt and grief.

I scrambled off of the window seat, almost falling to the floor in the process. I hurried out of my room and down the stairs. The soft strains of what sounded like a soap opera came from the bedroom down the hall.

I moved into the kitchen, searching for any signs that my mom had ventured out here this morning. Dishes in the sink? Crumbs on the counter? A banana missing from the bunch?

There was nothing.

I opened the pantry and pulled out bread and a bag of chips. I went about making a sandwich. Turkey with sharp cheddar and a spicy honey mustard that used to be Mom and Lacey's favorite. I added lettuce, tomato, and caramelized onion.

I cut it in two and placed it on the plate with a handful of chips. Grabbing a bottle of lemonade from the fridge, I made my way down the hall. The muted voices grew stronger, one asking, "How could you, Iris? And with my brother?"

I knocked softly on the door. There was no answer. I turned the handle and pushed the door open.

The room was dark, no light except for the glow from the television. My mom stared at the screen, but it was an unfocused stare, one that told me she had no idea what was actually going on in front of her. She didn't care if the shirtless man on-screen had just had his heart broken. She only wanted the numbness the show could provide.

"Hey, Mom," I said softly.

She blinked a few times and turned towards my voice. "Rowan."

Her voice was rusty, as if she hadn't used it in years. I started towards her, setting the plate and lemonade on her nightstand. "I made you a little something to eat. Can I open the curtains so you can see better?"

Mom shook her head, the movement slow as if she were sedated. "No. My head hurts. I don't want the light."

My gaze shifted to the bowl shoved to the far side of the nightstand. The pasta I'd made her for dinner last night had maybe a few bites missing. "You need to eat. You'll get sick if you don't."

She'd ended up in the hospital twice in the past six months after fainting spells. She'd lost so much weight, she was practically skin and bones. Whenever I'd tried to talk to Dad about it, he'd brush it off and tell me she needed time to heal. It didn't seem to me like she was healing. She was disappearing right in front of my eyes.

"Please, Mom," I urged.

Her eyes narrowed a fraction. "Leave."

I stiffened, my fingers curling into my palms. "Mom…"

She turned away from me, back to the screen. "I can't look at you."

The pang lighting along my heart was back, more vicious than ever, but I didn't say a thing. I couldn't. I didn't have any words to give. I didn't seem to have the ability to move either.

My mom's hands tightened in the blankets. "Every time I look at you, all I see is Lacey."

CHAPTER TWO

THE BACK DOOR SLAMMED AND I RAN ACROSS THE DECK, down the stairs. The breeze whipped my hair across my face as I charged for the trees, but I couldn't get any of it into my lungs. It was as if my ribs had tightened too much. It was impossible to let any air in.

The pine branches slapped against my arms as I ran down a path. It was dumb, so incredibly stupid, to run into a forest that you had no map for or knowledge of, but once I started, I couldn't seem to stop myself. My lungs and throat burned, but I welcomed the sensation.

It distracted me from the words wreaking havoc on my mind. *I can't look at you. All I see is Lacey.*

I choked back a sob, almost colliding with a tree. My feet tangled and I threw my hands out to catch my fall. The rough bark bit into my palms.

My chest heaved and my side cramped as I straightened. My gaze swept around, jumping from one thing to the next, trying to get my bearings.

It was breathtaking and that only made everything hurt more. The trees looked as if they were made of emeralds, and the mossy ground looked soft enough to take a nap on.

The sound of rushing water pulled me forward. I climbed up

an embankment as tears tracked down my cheeks. I eased my-self onto the ground and watched as the water rushed by below me, a mixture of deep blues and greens capped with white. It all swirled together, reminding me of the chaos that lived inside me, but more beautiful.

I pulled my knees to my chest and rocked myself back and forth. I focused on the sound of the water, letting it drown out the echoes of my mother's words. If it was this loud at the be-ginning of fall, I could only imagine what it was like when the snow melted off the mountains.

Lacey would've loved it. She would've demanded that we take picnics out here, invent stories about the faeries that surely lived in the hollowed logs in the forest, and built us a fort that would be hidden in the brush.

I could see it as clearly as if she were sitting right next to me. Her dark brown hair cascading down her back as she tipped her head back in laughter. My stomach hollowed out, the pain carv-ing its own home there.

The water wasn't loud enough. Nothing ever would be, not to drown out the pain of losing her.

"What are you doing out here? Don't you know a boundary when you see one?"

My head snapped up, and I scrambled away from the deep voice. The sun piercing through the trees blinded me for a mo-ment. I could only make out a form. Ripped jeans. A dark gray T-shirt pulled tight across a muscular chest. Tattoos that peeked out from underneath the sleeves.

"S-s-sorry. I didn't know this was private property."

He took a step forward, his face coming into view from be-hind the sunbeam. It was the kind of face that stole your breath and made you stupid. All sharp angles and hard planes. And eyes that were the lightest blue I'd ever seen. It was a complete juxtaposition to his hair that was so dark brown, it was almost black. Those almost angelic eyes sucker-punched me right in the chest. Because they held a pain that was so familiar, it felt like I was looking in a mirror.

"It's not private property," he gritted out.

"But you just said…"

His head tilted in a way similar to the blond guy's, as if he were looking at a pile of puzzle pieces, trying to figure out how they all went together. "Who are you?"

I looked around the forest, searching for a phantom some-one to save me from this handsome stranger's questions. "I don't think I should tell you my name."

The corner of his mouth kicked up. The action pulled on a scar on his lip just to the side of his cupid's bow. "Don't take candy out of the back of vans either, I'm guessing?"

"Stranger danger and all that."

Those ice-blue eyes lit as he took me in. "If you're concerned about safety, you probably shouldn't be out in the middle of the woods by yourself."

He had a very solid point, yet even with him hulking over me, I didn't want to leave. "Is it okay if I stay? Just for a little bit?"

The question seemed to take him by surprise. He took a half step back, eyes narrowing in on my face. They moved over my cheeks to my eyes and that was when he must've seen it, the remnants of my tears. I was sure my eyes were bloodshot and my cheeks red.

I didn't let myself wipe the evidence away. I was so tired of hiding what I was feeling around everyone. It was exhausting. For one brief moment, I simply wanted to *be*.

I wanted to listen to the water and soak the peace of this

place into my bones. To store it up so that I could carry it home with me. Maybe it would stay with me, tide me over until my mother had another outburst, or my father eventually forgot he had any daughters at all.

A muscle in his cheek ticked. "It's not a good idea. There are wild animals out here, sometimes hunters too."

"You're out here."

"I live here."

"In the woods?" Images of a makeshift shelter filled my mind.

"In my cabin. I know my way around here, know what to look out for. You don't."

I didn't know why I was trying to convince this rude guy to let me stay. Combative wasn't my usual M.O., but as I stared at him, I realized that I felt a little less alone. Just for a minute, I wasn't the girl who had lost her family six months ago. Lacey might've been dead, but Mom and Dad had pretty much left me by choice.

That sting had dulled when this guy stepped out of the trees. The reason made no sense. I gave my head a little shake.

"No, you refuse to leave?" he asked, his voice hardening around the edges.

That hardness cut. Again, the why made no sense. He was a stranger. I shouldn't care what he thought about me at all.

"I'm leaving." I started to push to my feet, my palm stinging as I pressed it to the ground to rise. I shook my hand trying to alleviate the bite of pain.

The guy's hand snaked out, catching my hand in his. The moment our skin touched, it was as if he'd burned me. A zing of electricity snapping at my skin.

He snatched his hand back so fast, he was a blur, horror filling his expression.

I stared at my palm. Small streaks of blood dotted the scrapes from the tree and little crescent-shaped fingernail marks cut across the flesh. Had our touch caused the scrapes to spark and burn? It didn't make sense.

I looked up to ask him if he'd felt something too, but he was gone.

CHAPTER THREE

I PADDED DOWN THE STAIRS, MY THICK, COZY SOCKS muffling my steps. I paused on the bottom step and listened. The quiet sounds of the TV still drifted from my parents' room.

I started for the kitchen. Pulling open the fridge, I surveyed the contents. There wasn't a lot left. Some things for sandwiches, a carton of eggs. I lifted the carton of milk and shook it. Not even enough for a bowl of cereal.

I grabbed the eggs and some cheese and moved to the counter. I whisked two eggs and poured them into a pan. As they cooked, I grated some cheese, sprinkling it over the top at just the right moment. When it was melted, I slipped them onto a plate.

I went back to the fridge, grabbing a soda and some salsa. At least I had caffeine. My life might be a total and complete disaster, but I had Diet Coke.

I sat down at the table and began to eat. I barely tasted the eggs, my mind drifting to the guy in the woods yesterday. I could've sworn I'd seen a sort of understanding in those ice-blue eyes, something that told me he knew the pain I'd been drowning in for the past six months.

The sound of the front door opening and closing drifted

through the house that felt more like a ghost town. Sneakers squeaked against the hardwood floors.

My dad appeared in the kitchen, startling when he saw me. "Rowan, I didn't know you were up."

"I didn't know you were home."

He certainly hadn't bothered to come up to my bedroom to let me know he was.

Dad moved to a cabinet, grabbing a glass and filling it with water. "I got home late last night and went for a run first thing. Didn't want to wake you."

The running was new, too. Sleek workout gear I'd never thought my dad would wear. Trendy joggers and one of those form-fitting, long-sleeved shirts.

"I probably wasn't asleep," I muttered. My hours of sleep were few and far between, peppered with nightmares and waking up in a cold sweat, calling out Lacey's name.

"Well, I couldn't have known that."

He could've. My parents used to always check in on me and Lacey when we were supposed to be asleep. They'd stealthily open our doors, peeking their heads in. Dad used to say, "Just want to make sure you're alive and breathing."

That familiar sting lit along my heart. Now, one of us wasn't alive and breathing, and I was the only daughter left. One that wasn't theirs by blood. I used to think that made me special—I had been a choice, not happenstance. But now, I wondered if it made me dispensable.

Dad cleared his throat. "First day of school tomorrow. Do you have everything you need?"

School. I couldn't wait. I'd take any excuse to escape the walls of this house that felt more like a haunted prison. The mother, who was more like a ghost than a living human, wandering the halls. Even when she never left her room, I could still feel her everywhere.

"We need groceries," I told him.

He straightened, pulling open the fridge. "Oh, I thought your mom—"

"She's not even eating. She barely leaves her bedroom. Do you really think she's going to drive to the grocery store?"

Dad turned to me, shutting the fridge door in the process. "You could have a little compassion for her—"

"I do have compassion. It's why I've been cooking for her every day. It's why I make myself go into that bedroom even when she says she can't bear to look at me."

"Rowan." The single word was a harsh plea. He squeezed his eyes closed for a brief moment. "I'll go to the store this afternoon before I head back to the city."

"You're leaving today?" I'd barely seen him and he was already disappearing, just like everyone else in my life. Sister, mother, boyfriend who couldn't deal with my grief.

"I have a meeting first thing in the morning."

I didn't say a word. I wouldn't beg him to stay. It would only hurt more when he left anyway.

Dad grabbed the notepad and pen from their spot by the phone. "Here. Write down what you think you'll need for the week. I'll leave you some cash in case anything else pops up. You can take Mom's car if you need to run errands."

If he'd handed me her keys, I would've dropped them. I had my license, but I hadn't driven since before the accident. It didn't matter that I hadn't been the one behind the wheel, I couldn't handle the fear that swamped me each and every time I'd tried.

My hand instinctively went to the scar along my ribs. The raised flesh was less angry now, but it would forever be a reminder of that night. The doctors didn't know how I'd survived. It had taken hours for fire and rescue to get me and Lacey out of the car. They said I should've bled out. Somehow, I hadn't. Some days, I wished I had.

The doorbell rang, startling me from the morbid walk down memory lane. We'd met a couple of neighbors when we were moving in, but no one had come by the house. I hadn't ever heard the doorbell.

Dad and I both froze for a moment. "Let's see who that is."

I wanted to tell him he could handle it for once. I didn't want the responsibility of pasting on a smile for strangers. Instead, I pushed to my feet and followed him to the front door.

He opened the door to reveal a man and the blond guy I'd seen out my window yesterday. He was even more striking close-up. That blond hair ruffled in an effortless, artful way. His eyes were a deep blue that reminded me of the water in the creek I'd seen yesterday. An angular jaw and rosy lips completed a look that I was sure made him popular with the girls in town.

The man beside him held out a hand to my father. "Mr. Caldwell, I'm Mason Pierce. I'm on the town council, and when I heard you had a daughter my son's age, I volunteered us to bring your welcome basket."

I took in the basket in the blond's hands. It was full to bursting with what looked like pamphlets and gourmet snacks.

The guy held it out to me. "Welcome to Cloverdale. I'm Holden."

Holden. It fit him. "Nice to meet you. I'm Rowan."

I reached out, taking the basket from his outstretched hands. Our fingers brushed as I did, and a shock of electricity sparked between us, freezing me to the spot for a moment.

Holden's eyes flared, seeming to swirl and change colors for a moment.

I pulled the basket towards me, unsure of what to say. There must have been static electricity in the air around here.

Dad released Mr. Pierce's hand. "Please, call me Bruce. Thank you for coming by. I'm sure it'll be nice for Rowan to have a familiar face at school tomorrow."

I fought the wince that tried to surface. The last thing I wanted was this guy taking pity on me.

His eyes scanned my face, seeming to search for something. "I'd be happy to show you around to your classes."

Mr. Pierce grinned. "Holden is student council president, so he knows all the ins and outs to Cloverdale High."

It was fitting, this golden boy being student council president. He was probably captain of the football team and dating the head cheerleader, too.

I tried to smile but knew it probably came out as more of a grimace. "Thank you. I appreciate it, but I got a tour earlier this week, so I know where I'm going."

Holden frowned, lines bracketing his perfect mouth. "Okay, well, I'll save you a seat at lunch then."

"Sure, thanks." I wouldn't be taking him up on that. Holden's beauty meant that he was surely the center of a lot of attention. I wanted nothing but to fade into the background.

"So where did you guys move from?" Mason asked.

"Baltimore," Dad answered. "I took a job with an accounting firm in Seattle."

Mason let out a whistle. "That's a hell of a commute."

"Unfortunately, it's forcing me to spend most of my week in the city."

"Well, if your wife or Rowan need anything, my card is in the basket. I'm always happy to help."

Dad put an arm around my shoulders. "There certainly is something to this small-town thing."

I almost shuddered at the contact. How long had it been since my dad had touched me? A hug? A pat on the shoulder? Anything? I think it had been Lacey's funeral.

Tears burned the back of my throat. "Nice to meet you," I whispered and hurried away from the entry. I needed space. To breathe. Anything that would erase the pain eating me alive.

CHAPTER FOUR

I LOOKED UP AT THE SKY AS I STEPPED OUT THE FRONT door. The sun had decided that the first day of school was the perfect time to hide behind clouds so thick it barely felt like day at all. I really hoped it wasn't an omen.

I set down my backpack and slid on my jacket. No, not my jacket. It had been Lacey's. A leather creation she'd scrimped and saved for months to buy. She could pull off the edgy look with ease. On me it looked a little forced, but I didn't care. I'd wear anything if it meant feeling a little closer to her. Especially on the first day at a new school.

I wound my way through our neighborhood and towards town. The downtown area was quaint with old brick buildings and carefully curated storefronts. There was even an old-fashioned soda shop with a huge jukebox and teal booths.

Maybe I would opt to do homework there after classes, if it wasn't crowded. Anything that would prolong going back to the ghost house. Dad had left as soon as he'd stocked the fridge and shoved money into my hands. He'd affixed Mason Pierce's business card to the front of the fridge and told me to call him if I had any issues.

He didn't want to know about whatever problems waited

for him at home. What would he do if Mom starved herself to death? Would he even notice?

My fingers curled around the ties of my bracelet. I focused on the motion, twisting and untwisting the cord around my finger. It had become almost a meditation of sorts, something to keep me grounded when all I wanted to do was float away.

I turned the corner as I skirted downtown, the high school coming into view. The brick of the buildings fit with the rest of town. It wasn't big, but it wasn't small either. Somewhere in between. The woman who had given me a tour had told me that the students who went there weren't just from Cloverdale but the whole county.

That knowledge had helped me breathe a bit easier. The more students, the easier it would be to disappear into the background. But as I watched cars pour into the parking lot and buses come to a stop in front of the main building, my heart stuttered in my chest.

I pulled the cord tighter around my finger. I could do this. No one knew me here. I had a completely fresh slate.

I crossed the street and made my way through the parking lot. The cars were a total mixed bag. Some looked as if they were held together with duct tape and a prayer, some were the typical used-but-in-good-condition sedans, and a few were more luxury vehicles. I even spotted a brand-new Range Rover.

I kept my head down as I walked towards the entrance, only stealing a few furtive glances to try to pick out the groups. I was hoping for casual friendships. The kind where you sat together at lunch and assemblies but never actually discussed more than homework and the latest gossip.

I needed to find that middle-of-the-road group. The one

that nobody paid any attention to because they simply blended. Those were my people.

My gaze caught on a group of girls who stood by the front doors. They all seemed to circle one girl in the center. She was tall and lean, with long blonde hair that looked so shiny she should've been in a shampoo commercial. She tossed her hair over her shoulder and laughed.

The sound was meant to be carefree, but I could hear the lie in it. There was a slightly false tinge to the vibration that I recognized because I heard it in my father's laugh and in my own. I couldn't help but wonder what the girl was hiding behind that fake laugh.

I turned my focus to the doors, pulling one open. The halls were already filling with people, and I did my best to dodge around them as I moved towards my locker. I breathed a sigh of relief when I reached it without getting lost or knocking into anyone.

I spun the dial on the lock and it popped free. Swinging my backpack around, I unloaded the notebooks and binders I wouldn't need until after lunch. I pulled out my schedule, scanning it for what felt like the hundredth time. First up was astronomy, then pre-calculus, and finally art. I'd be holding it together until art. God, I hoped that the teacher was good.

I was so focused on my schedule, I didn't feel the shift. Typically, I was tuned to that change in tone, always on the lookout for those soft whispers. The ones people thought you couldn't hear but that were worse than if they'd screamed whatever they were saying.

I stole a quick glance to the side. A group of three girls and two boys were speaking in hushed voices, but every so often, they would all look my way. I turned back to my locker, hoping to hide my red cheeks behind the metal door. I took a steadying breath. They probably didn't get a whole lot of new kids around here. They were just curious.

"Her sister was killed in the accident. Can you imagine?" A female voice drifted down the hall.

My breathing picked up, and I scrambled to zip my backpack up.

"I heard it took them hours to get her out of the car. She should've died," another girl said.

I could see them out of the corner of my eye, that same group of girls who'd been at the front of the school. They stared blatantly at me, not caring at all if I noticed. It wasn't the act itself that bothered me, it was how it made me feel. It was as if their gazes scraped at my skin, leaving me raw and bloodied.

"That's awful. You'd never be the same," a brunette girl murmured.

My ribs tightened around my lungs, cutting off my air supply. I needed out, away from their eyes and words. I slammed my locker closed and hurried down the hall. I dodged people left and right, a few muttering curses in my wake when they dropped a schedule or book.

I hurried farther into the depths of the school, looking for anything that resembled respite. Most of the classrooms were lit and already filling with people, but there was one up ahead that looked dark.

My vision went hazy as I struggled to get any sort of air into my lungs. Memories flashed in my mind. The feel of Lacey's hand in mine. The pain in my side. The darkness stealing me away. Shouts and lights. The pain.

I yanked the door open to the darkened classroom and stumbled inside. As I did, I slammed into a hard form and gasped. Then I was falling.

CHAPTER FIVE

"**S**HIT!"

The voice sounded far away but hands caught me under my arms, settling me on a hard plastic chair. "Just breathe."

The voice seemed a little closer now. I blinked a few times, my eyes adjusting to the low light of the classroom. The guy in front of me came into focus. He had sandy brown hair that was shaved on the sides and longer on top. His hazel eyes seemed to swirl with concern.

My cheeks heated. "S-sorry."

"It's all right. Nice and easy now. Follow me." The guy lifted his hand as he inhaled and lowered it as he exhaled.

I tried to follow, but each breath hurt. Oxygen disguised as razor blades. I focused on the guy's hand. He had a broad, callused palm. Instead of thinking about the burn in my chest, I wondered what put those calluses there.

A warmth spread through me, relaxing my muscles as I pictured him building a house with his bare hands. I blinked a few more times and realized I was breathing normally.

"Thank you. I'm so sorry. I don't normally..." I wasn't even sure how to finish that sentence.

He waved me off. "Don't worry about it. First days are rough."

I bit my lip and nodded. Let him think I was a delicate flower rocked by first-day jitters, not a basket case haunted by the feel of her sister's hand as she slipped from this earth.

He held out a hand. "I'm Lucas."

My hand trembled slightly as I reached out to shake his. "Rowan."

My lips parted as our skin touched. Warmth bloomed in my palm as that now, somewhat familiar spark skated along my skin.

Lucas jerked back his hand. "Shit. Sorry, I—static electricity."

"Seems to be a continual problem around here."

His gaze snapped to mine. "What?"

"Nothing," I muttered. "I should probably find my first class."

"Sure…what do you have?"

"Astronomy."

Lucas grinned and it was devastating. It made the gold in his eyes dance. "Me too. I can show you the way."

"Thanks." It was all I could think to say. Brushing off the guy who'd kept me from having a panic attack seemed incredibly rude.

I pushed to my feet, but Lucas still towered over me, broad shoulders cutting into a lean waist. His muscular form was that of a swimmer's, and I had the sudden urge to ask, to know more about him. I kept my mouth firmly closed.

"So, you moved from Baltimore?"

I glanced up at Lucas as we walked into the hall, joining the slightly less crowded swarm of students. "Information really travels fast around here, doesn't it?"

He shrugged, but sympathy filled his expression. I knew without him saying a word that he too knew about the accident and Lacey. "Small towns usually have a pretty strong gossip system, and since not a lot happens here, people are pretty desperate for anything to talk about."

I twirled my bracelet tie around my finger. "How long till they stop talking?"

"It depends on how long it takes for someone to do something scandalous."

"Would it be wrong of me to pray for a teenage pregnancy or maybe an affair?"

Lucas barked out a laugh. "It would only make you a little evil."

The corners of my mouth curved up. "Evil's my middle name."

"I doubt that."

I looked up, meeting his hazel stare. "How do you know?"

His steps slowed. "Just a feeling, I guess."

He opened the door to the classroom for me, and I stepped through. I hovered just inside, unsure where exactly to go. The teacher was focused on a stack of paperwork on her desk and didn't even look up.

I jumped as a hand touched my elbow. Lucas inclined his head towards a row of desks. "You can sit next to me if you want."

I could've kissed him for taking the pressure off of me deciding where to sit. "Sure. Thanks."

He smiled and led me down the row. Two other guys sat towards the middle of the room. Lucas fist bumped each of them. "Ridge, Jack, this is Rowan. It's her first day, and I'm not sure our school is making the best impression."

Jack smiled at me as he brushed his red hair out of his eyes. "Nice to meet you, Rowan. I promise, nobody actually bites."

Ridge scowled at the group of girls clustered around someone on the other side of the classroom. "Some people can be real bitches. Just ignore them."

The way Ridge's eyes narrowed on the blonde girl I'd seen earlier, I knew they'd been talking about me before I'd arrived.

She shifted slightly, giggling as a guy tugged on a strand of her hair. He grinned devilishly at her, his green eyes dancing.

He was gorgeous, with buzzed dark brown hair and scruff around his jaw. He had a kind of confidence that clearly drew girls to him. His gaze drifted away from the blonde and locked with mine.

I sucked in a sharp breath. I wanted to look away, but I couldn't seem to force myself. Yes, there was charm and cockiness there, but somehow, I knew that underneath it all, there was pain. In the same way I'd sensed it in the guy in the woods.

A hand touched my lower back, warmth and comfort sinking into the muscles there. I had the bizarre desire to burrow into it. I blinked a few times, clearing my mind and pulling away from the other guy's intense stare.

Lucas looked down at me with concern in his gaze again, his hand still on my back. "Are you okay?"

No, I wasn't okay. My sister was dead. I was in a new school where everyone knew my secrets. I kept sensing things about strangers, feeling pulled towards them when I should have been running in the opposite direction.

"Yes," I croaked.

If we were staying in Cloverdale, I needed to become a better liar.

CHAPTER SIX

I EASED THE STACK OF BOOKS INTO MY LOCKER AND PINCHED the bridge of my nose. By the time I'd made it to art class, my head had been pounding, a steady thrum at my temples and between my eyes. All I wanted was quiet, away from the whispers and probing stares.

I pulled out the notebooks I'd need for my afternoon classes and slipped them into my backpack. Grabbing my lunch, I turned to survey my options. I guessed it would be frowned upon to eat in the library, but I'd seen a tiny courtyard off to the side of it that might be empty.

I started down the hall, only to hear my name being called. I winced but kept walking. Hopefully, whoever it was would give up and turn around.

A hand caught my elbow. "Rowan, hey."

I turned to see the golden boy grinning down at me. "Hey, Holden."

"Where are you going? The cafeteria is the other way."

My fingers tightened around my lunch bag. "I've had a little too much people for one day. I was going to eat in that courtyard."

Holden grimaced, and I knew he had heard all the talk circulating about me. "We have to eat in the cafeteria. If you get caught elsewhere, you'll get detention."

My shoulders slumped and I felt the sudden urge to cry.

Holden gripped my shoulders, his touch somehow managing to be gentle and firm at the same time. "It'll be okay, promise. You can sit with me and my friends. No one will bug you if you're with us."

My fingers curled into my palms, digging into the skin there. That bite of pain helped keep the tears at bay. "Thanks."

"Of course."

Holden led the way towards double doors at the end of the hall. The closer we got, the more the din of voices grew. With each step, I tried to shore up my armor and cement my mask into place. The less I reacted, the sooner everyone would forget about me altogether.

Holden opened one of the doors and ushered me inside. My gaze swept over the cafeteria. The tables were fairly large and circular, with enough seating for at least fifteen people. Some looked up as I entered, but far more stayed focused on their own conversations and meals.

That changed the moment Holden placed a hand on my lower back. I felt a prickle of electricity jump from his hand into the muscles at my back. It wasn't the same as the spark I'd felt when he'd handed me the gift basket, this was more like a low hum of awareness.

The buzz of conversations quieted as Holden gently pushed me forward. He pointed to a table in the center of the room. "That's our spot."

Of course, it had to be the one where the entire room could see us. I swallowed, trying to clear some of the dryness in my throat. Girls and guys alike stared as we walked by. I did my best to focus only on the floor in front of me.

We came to a stop at the table, and people shifted to create more space. Holden's hand didn't move from my back. "Guys, this is Rowan."

I forced myself to lift my gaze to the table's occupants. I met Lucas' warm, hazel stare, except it was a little harder than I'd seen this morning, and it was zeroed in on Holden's hand on my back. My cheeks heated. "Hi, everyone."

I quickly slid into an empty seat and Holden followed.

A blonde girl sitting directly across from me beamed. "Hi, Rowan. I'm Cassidy, everyone calls me Cass. Nice to meet you." The two guys I had met in astronomy, Ridge and Jack, sat on either side of her.

"You too," I said, trying for a warm smile but falling way short.

"Glad you made it through the gauntlet," Jack chimed in.

"Barely," I muttered.

Ridge shook his head. "Ignore the idiots."

Holden pointed to the two other guys. "This is Lucas and Keene."

"We've met." There was almost a slight growl to Lucas' words. It didn't fit with the person who had been so gentle with me this morning.

I cleared my throat, as if that could ease the tension at the table. "We have astronomy together, with Ridge and Jack."

"That's great," Cassidy said, still smiling as if she were oblivious to the stare Lucas was sending Holden's way.

I looked at Keene, trying to mirror Cassidy's easy grin. "Nice to meet you too."

He studied me for a moment. It wasn't angry exactly, more like cold calculation. As if he were assessing every last thing about me with those ice-blue eyes.

Lucas elbowed him in the ribs. "Don't be a dick."

Keene grimaced. "Nice to meet you."

Somehow, I didn't quite believe that.

"So," Cassidy said, interrupting the assessment. "How is the first day?"

Jack wrapped an arm around Cassidy and kissed her temple. "Wrong question."

She looked up at him. "Why?"

"Because Sadie and her bitch squad are making it miserable."

Cassidy's eyes hardened as she turned her focus to another table. "What is wrong with that girl?"

I followed her line of sight and found the blonde who must have been Sadie perched on the lap of the handsome, green-eyed guy's lap.

"Whatever it is, Anson seems to eat it up," Ridge muttered.

"Because he's a fool," Holden gritted out.

My gaze jumped to Holden. I'd never heard that aggression in his tone before, and the glare accompanying it had me wanting to create a bit more distance between us.

Cassidy shook her head. "Just ignore the mean girls. They'll move on to other prey soon."

I wouldn't wish their attention on anyone, but I didn't want it on me either.

"I don't know about that, Cass," Lucas said. "She's too pretty and *Holden* just made her a target."

Holden stiffened next to me. "You have a problem, Lucas?"

"Yes—"

"What do you mean, made me a target?" I interrupted. The last thing I wanted was a bullseye on my back.

Cassidy winced. "Lots of girls want Holden's attention, and he doesn't exactly invite many people to sit with us."

What was this? Some sort of small-town mafia? I didn't

want any part of some weird, invite-only table that would make all the girls at this school hate me.

"It wouldn't have been bad if he hadn't walked you through the damn cafeteria," Lucas grumbled.

"Lucas…." Everything about the single word was a warning.

A girl with dark brown hair and golden skin lowered herself into the seat next to Holden. Except it wasn't really a full seat, more like half of one, and it put her almost sitting in Holden's lap. "What'd I miss?" Her gaze narrowed a fraction as it landed on me. "New girl."

"Old girl," I shot back.

Ridge stifled a laugh by pressing his mouth to Cassidy's shoulder. I waited for Jack to smack him or something for practically kissing who I assumed was his girlfriend, but Jack didn't seem to be bothered at all.

Cassidy just shook her head. "That welcoming charmer is Jasmine."

I nodded but didn't say anything else. I'd had enough of stares and judgment today. The headache pulsing behind my eyes thrummed harder.

Lucas moved in closer so that our thighs were touching. The warmth of that one, tiny connection seemed to soothe the worst of my fraying edges, almost as if he were pulling the anxiety and exhaustion from me.

He sent me a warm smile. "It'll get better, promise."

Jasmine rolled her eyes. "Enough with all the touchy-feely stuff."

"Jaz," Holden warned.

She ducked her head. "Sorry."

A commotion sounded at the table next to us. Sadie shrieked as the guy I now knew was named Anson tossed her over his shoulder and smacked her butt. "I thought you wanted me to walk you to class."

"Not like this, Anson. Put me down."

Her tone and huge grin told me that was the last thing she wanted him to do.

"I'll put you down." He heaved her into the air, sending her flying at one of his friends.

She giggled as the other boy caught her.

"I don't know what gets into him sometimes," Cass muttered.

Anson's gaze locked with mine, searing through me. He sent a wink my way and strode out of the cafeteria. My reaction was visceral—a hatred of that tiny action so fierce, it felt as if my insides were burning. Because everything in me knew with complete certainty that it was fake, a façade that Anson put on for his friends and classmates. And something about that clawed at my soul.

CHAPTER SEVEN

I KEPT MY EYES CAST LOW, TRYING TO SURREPTITIOUSLY take in my surroundings. The classroom was set up with at least a dozen lab tables, odd since this was a religion class, but everything about my experiences at Cloverdale High had been less than normal.

My gaze caught on a familiar figure walking towards the room. Cassidy paused in the doorway, linking her arms around Ridge's neck and letting him kiss her long and slow. My mouth fell open. Was I losing my mind? She'd been kissing Jack at lunch.

"Slut," Sadie said behind the guise of a cough.

Cass didn't seem bothered in the slightest. She gave Ridge another quick peck and then came down from her tiptoes. She shot Sadie a wolfish grin as she passed. "Green really isn't a good look on you. Clashes with your complexion."

Sadie turned beet red and glared at Cassidy.

As Cass caught sight of me, her smile widened as she slid into the chair next to me. "I was hoping we'd have a class together. Unfortunately, this one can be boring as hell."

I was actually somewhat looking forward to it. Learning about religions and customs from all over the world sounded like an escape.

Cass chuckled. "I can see your doubt, but trust me, Ms.

Angler just makes us read from the book each day. She only lectures for like ten minutes."

That did sound boring, but I was a fast reader, so maybe I could get some of my other homework done in this class too. "There could be worse things, I guess."

"For sure."

I couldn't help glancing at Sadie and then back to Cass. Sadie and two of her friends were whispering furiously.

"Are you and Ridge dating?" The question just popped out before I had a chance to stop it. "I'm sorry, that was rude and totally none of my business. Ignore me."

Cass chuckled. "I don't think asking if I'm dating someone is rude. Especially if we're going to be friends, which I have a feeling we are."

A hint of warmth flitted through me at her words. Cassidy was kind and took no shit from anyone. Exactly the type of friend I'd be lucky to have.

"I am dating Ridge. And Jack. And Cooper, but he's a year older and is in college now."

I knew my jaw had slackened. "W-what?"

Cassidy burst out laughing. "Oh my gosh, you should see your face right now."

"I, uh, I mean, good for you."

She bumped my shoulder with hers. "I know, right? I'm a lucky girl. And it's not totally abnormal around here."

"To date multiple people?" I guessed it wasn't that odd. People at my old school would've just called it hooking up.

Cassidy shifted in her seat. "The community I live in, it's typical for some women to date, and even marry, more than one guy."

"Oh." I wasn't sure what else to say to that. "Everyone at lunch…?"

"We all live together. Not in the same house or anything. Mason, Holden's dad, owns this massive piece of property at the foot of the mountains. We all have homes out there."

"Cult," one of the girls with Sadie hissed.

Cass rolled her eyes. "Some folks around town think it's weird. Some will say nasty things, but for the most part, people are cool about it. We're just a tight-knit community, like an extended family."

I couldn't imagine being in that kind of relationship, but I hated that any of the people I'd met at lunch might receive judgment and derision. They were the only people who'd been truly kind and welcoming to me today. Well, everyone except Jasmine.

I shrugged. "It's not like you're hurting anyone. I say do whatever makes you happy."

"Me too. And trust me, Jack, Ridge, and Cooper make me *very* happy."

Sadie made a scoffing noise. "They'll get tired of you, Cassidy. It's only a matter of time."

"Your jealousy is showing again," Cass sang back.

I tried to cover my laugh with a cough, but Sadie's eyes narrowed on me. I quickly averted my gaze, focusing on my textbook.

Cass tracked Sadie's gaze and muttered a curse. "You might want to avoid her for a while."

"I'm trying to. What's her deal anyway?"

"Sadie may be a bitch to me, but she's been angling for a lunch invitation from Holden for years. She's pissed you got that on day one."

"It was a pity invite," I whispered. "He knows I just moved to town and don't know anyone."

"I wouldn't be so sure about that. We've had new people before, and they've never been invited to sit with us. Holden's not big on outsiders. And Lucas was right about one thing—it brought you to the attention of Sadie and her crew."

Great. The only potential friends I'd made at Cloverdale might have just put me in the crosshairs.

CHAPTER EIGHT

I STUFFED THE LAST OF MY BOOKS INTO MY BACKPACK AND slung it over my shoulder. The weight of everything nearly toppled me over. The walk to school hadn't been bad, but with what felt like one hundred pounds on my back, that walk might seem a little longer going home. Someone should suggest e-books to the school board. Then the students wouldn't be diagnosed with scoliosis by the end of the year.

I shut my locker and twisted the lock. Pinching the bridge of my nose, I blinked a few times. The headache that had disappeared after lunch was back in full force. All I wanted now was a hot bath, some mac and cheese, and bed.

I made my way down the mostly empty hall. Classrooms had emptied with a speed that had my head spinning. Apparently, sticking around school wasn't the cool thing to do. That was just fine with me. It meant I could take my time and have my solitude as I walked home.

I stopped just before I reached the front doors, familiar voices catching my attention from around the corner.

"She has no idea what she is," Holden hissed. "You can't just dump something like that on her."

"She needs to know eventually. It's not like you can hide this forever. If we're both feeling the pull, it means she's powerful. She needs to be protected," Lucas argued.

"Dad's handling it," Holden said firmly.

"Forgive me if I don't want to put all my trust in your dad when she's my—"

"Hey, Rowan," Keene said, cutting Lucas off as he poked his head around the corner.

I let out a little shriek, stumbling back a step. "Don't do that."

He grinned. "Sorry. I saw your reflection in the glass." He pointed to the doors, and sure enough, there I was, caught red-handed eavesdropping.

Holden smiled at me, but it was forced. "I was just going to look for you. I wanted to give you a ride home."

I adjusted my backpack, trying to relieve a bit of the pressure on my shoulders. "That's all right. I'm fine walking."

"But you don't have to. Your house is on my way home."

"Really, it's fine—"

Lucas slipped the backpack from my shoulders. "This thing weighs about a ton. You really shouldn't be carrying it home."

Keene shook his head. "Just give up now. They're both stubborn assholes when they're determined to help."

"And what about you? Are you only a stubborn asshole when you're staring me down in cafeterias, or did I pass your weird test?"

Lucas barked out a laugh as he swung my backpack onto his own shoulder. "She already knows you so well."

A hint of pink touched Keene's cheeks. "I needed to see what you were about."

"Worried I'm a serial killer?"

The corner of his mouth twitched, making those pale blue eyes of his almost seem to sparkle. "You might be, or some sort of other evil mastermind. That cute and innocent thing you have going on would be a good cover."

Now it was my turn to blush. "Don't go exposing me now. How will I go on my murderous rampage of the football team and cheer squad, if you do?"

Keene smiled fully and it had my stomach doing gymnastics. "I think I like you."

Holden shook his head and looked at Lucas. "It's truly a miracle. Do you have a camera? We should mark this moment for posterity."

Lucas pulled out his cell phone and snapped a picture of Keene. Keene dove for the phone, doing his best to yank it out of Lucas' hand. "You're such a douche."

Holden moved closer to me. "Sorry about all this. We're not usually such a mess."

"That's all right. It's nice that guys are so at ease with each other."

He chuckled. "At ease is one way to describe it."

I shuffled my feet as Lucas and Keene continued to struggle for the phone. "What were you guys talking about when I walked up?"

Holden's expression blanked. "What do you mean?"

"You said something about someone being powerful, not knowing what they were."

"Oh, that. Lucas' little sister is studying martial arts with my dad and Lucas. She has no idea how powerful she is or what she can do. Dad needs to have a talk with her because she kicked some poor kid's ass at the middle school last week."

I couldn't help it, I laughed. "Sounds like someone I want to know."

"Definitely," Holden agreed.

"Got it," Keene cheered, holding up the device.

Lucas snatched it from his grasp. "And now you don't."

"Come on, knuckleheads." Holden motioned us towards the doors. "Let's get Rowan home. I don't want her mom to worry."

I could've told them that her worrying was an impossibility, that she probably wouldn't notice if I didn't come home for weeks, but I kept my mouth closed.

Keene bumped my shoulder with his. "Let's go, evil mastermind."

"Careful, I could be plotting your demise."

"Naw, you like me too much."

I snorted. "It's a shame you have such a lack of confidence."

Lucas fell into step on my other side. "It really is."

Holden held out a key fob, and the lights on a brand-new truck flashed. He grabbed the back of Lucas' neck. "You're up front with me."

Lucas opened his mouth, as if he was about to argue, then shut it and nodded.

"You're stuck with me," Keene chirped.

"You're taking your life in your hands, but that's your choice."

"As long as Lucas has your potential weapons stashed in that backpack of yours, I think I'm safe."

I climbed into the back seat of the truck and grinned at Keene when he appeared on the other side. "No self-respecting evil mastermind only has weapons in her bag."

"You're screwed," Lucas called from the front seat as Holden started the engine.

Keene just laughed and leaned over to buckle his seat belt. I was doing the same, and as I straightened, our hands brushed. That now familiar sparking sensation lit up the side of my arm and the whole world seemed to fade around me. I could only hear the beating of my heart—no, two hearts.

"Rowan, are you okay?" Holden's voice jerked me out of my haze.

"Sorry. That was weird. Like I couldn't hear for a second."

Holden gave me a tight smile. "Long day with lots of loud voices. You probably just need some rest."

"Probably." But the suggestion had me realizing that I felt better than I had since lunch. My headache was gone and so was the bone-deep fatigue.

It was the laughter. I stilled as the town blurred past my window. I hadn't laughed since…I was with Lacey. Six months and not even a sitcom episode had startled a giggle out of me. Today was the first time.

CHAPTER NINE

LUCAS HANDED ME MY BACKPACK, AND I HOISTED IT over my shoulder. "Thanks again for the ride."

"No problem. We'll pick you up tomorrow morning around quarter to eight," Holden said.

"You don't have to—"

Lucas shook his head. "Resistance is futile."

I shifted in place as I thought about what Cassidy had said earlier today, that being friends with these guys would put attention and focus on me. But as I looked up and swept my gaze over the guys, I knew I wouldn't be able to keep my distance. They were kind when I'd desperately needed it, but it was more.

Just driving from school to my house, I felt lighter, as if they'd taken a little of the weight I carried every day. I felt safe with them, like nothing bad could happen to me as long as they were around.

It was ridiculous. I knew better than most that bad things could happen anywhere, anytime. But I didn't want to give up this little glimmer of hope that lit when I was around Holden, Lucas, and even Keene.

"Okay. I'll see you tomorrow."

Holden grinned. "Tomorrow."

Lucas jumped out of the truck. "Wait, give me your phone."

I slid it out of my pocket. I didn't know why I even had it with me. No one called. My friends had stopped reaching out months ago. My boyfriend had lasted less than thirty days after the accident before he'd gotten tired of drowning in my grief. He hadn't even had the courtesy to end things with me. He'd simply stopped calling, and one day at school, I'd seen him with his tongue down Clara King's throat.

"Rowan, you okay?" Lucas asked as he slid the phone from my fingers.

I forced my mouth to curve. "Sorry, just spacing. Long day."

He nodded but didn't look overly convinced. "I'm putting all our numbers in here, and I just texted myself so we'll have yours."

"And what if I didn't want you guys to have my number?"

"Too late now," Keene called from the truck.

Lucas moved in closer as he handed me back my phone, so close that I could feel the heat coming off his body. It was the same comforting warmth that always seemed to flow from him. When I reached for my phone, he didn't let go. "Call us if you need anything. We're only a few minutes away."

"Okay." The single word was soft. I wouldn't call. They were already saving me more than they knew.

"I mean it." There was the slightest growl to Lucas' words.

"She gets it, Luc," Holden chided.

Lucas shot him a glare and turned back to me, pulling me into a hug. The move happened so fast, I didn't have time to react. His larger form engulfed mine, his arms wrapping around me. That now familiar warmth swallowing me whole.

Something in me eased at the contact, my muscles loosening and those pangs of pain that always racked my heart easing a little. Lucas bent his head so his lips were at my ear. "You aren't alone."

Everything burned. My throat. The back of my eyes. My chest. How did he know the exact thing that I needed to hear?

Holden coughed and Lucas released me. "We'll see you tomorrow."

"Tomorrow," I muttered and started towards the house.

I didn't look back at the truck but didn't hear the engine start up until I'd closed and locked the door. I let my backpack drop to the floor and listened. The rumble of the truck engine faded in the distance. There was a tugging sensation in my chest. As much as Lucas' words were kind, they weren't true. I was completely alone now.

The hum of the television drifted down the hall. I sighed and started towards it. I'd left Mom a sandwich in the fridge for lunch and could only hope that she'd eaten it.

I knocked softly on the door. There was no answer. I slowly opened the door.

The room was even darker than normal, whatever TV show she had on wasn't bright enough to illuminate much. I froze as I stepped inside. My mom was curled on her side facing the door. Her body shook with violent sobs, yet she didn't make a sound.

There was only one word I could use to describe it…ravaged. Her pain was a living, breathing thing. It poured out of her and wrapped around me, almost taking me to my knees.

"Mom?" I croaked.

"Get out!" she wailed.

Instead, I took a step forward. "Please, let me help. Do you want me to call Dad?"

"I don't want anything from you. If we'd never brought you home, Lacey would still be here."

Each one of her words sliced across my skin. Not fatal, but meant to inflict as much pain as possible.

46

"Mom," I whispered.

"Don't call me that! You're not my daughter. Lacey was my daughter. And she's gone." The crying started in earnest again, shuddering sobs racking through her.

I leaned down, placing a hand on her back. She shoved at me, making me stumble back a few steps.

"Get out!"

I fled up the stairs to my bedroom. My hand trembled as I opened the door. My whole body was shaking. I barely made it to my bed before collapsing. It wasn't until my pillow grew damp that I realized I was crying.

Every time I thought I'd cried out everything inside me, there was still more—an infinite pool of pain to draw from. I curled into a ball, the hand with my bracelets pressing into the side of my face. "I need you, Lace."

There was no answer. Never was. Because I was alone.

An animal howled in the distance, the sound it made speaking right to my soul.

CHAPTER TEN

I LIFTED MY DIET COKE AND RESTED THE CAN ON ONE EYE and then the other. Between the crying and some sort of animal party in the forest behind our house last night, my sleep had been nil. My brain and face were paying the price. I could only hope that none of my teachers would call on me today, and that somehow the puffiness in my eyes would magically disappear by the time I got to school.

Even if my mind suddenly cleared and my face went back to normal, the ache in my chest would still be there. The pain of my mother's words swirled with the grief of missing Lacey, mixing with something else I couldn't identify exactly. A sort of tugging that left me wanting to gasp for breath.

I lifted the can off my eye and took a sip. I'd need at least a dozen more if I was going to get through today. I hadn't bothered making Mom a sandwich today, not when the one from yesterday still sat in the fridge, untouched.

I tapped out a text on my phone.

Me: *Mom isn't doing well. You might want to come home and check on her.*

Three little dots appeared and then disappeared again.

Dad: *She's grieving. Give her time.*

Time? If we gave her much more time, she was going to waste away to nothing.

I didn't bother responding to his text. He wouldn't care, no matter what I said. I couldn't force him to open his eyes and see the truth. He was living with his head in the sand with his new, three-hundred-dollar haircut.

My phone buzzed, and I fought the urge to throw it at the wall.

Lucas: *Your chariot awaits.*

I stared at the screen for a moment and briefly considered running away. I squashed the idea. One year. Less than that. It was all I had to get through before I could go to college and never look back. At least I knew there was a college fund in my name. It would pay for wherever I wanted to go.

Maybe I'd go somewhere overseas. I'd never been to Scotland, but it looked beautiful. Those lush green landscapes and majestic castles. I'd start investigating options tonight. If I could hold that image in my head of freedom, of leaving everything behind and truly becoming someone new, I could make it through this year.

Lucas: *You okay, Rowan?*

I hurried to type out a response.

Me: *Be out in a sec.*

I lifted my Diet Coke and chugged its contents. I left my empty bowl in the sink and grabbed my backpack. As I hefted it over my shoulder, I mentally thanked Holden for pushing the giving-me-a-ride issue.

I headed out the front door, locking it behind me. Keene hung out the back window of the truck. "Did you miss me?"

I couldn't help but chuckle. "I've been counting down the seconds until I'd see you again. How did you know?"

"Because I'm a catch and you're not stupid." There was a

commotion in the cab and Keene cursed. "That was uncalled for, Luc."

The petulant tone only had me smiling wider as I climbed into the back of the truck. "I need a ladder to get into this thing."

Keene reached out a hand and pulled me in. There was no deafening spark this time, but there was a little trill of sensation along my palm. "Thanks," I muttered, pulling off my backpack and setting it at my feet.

Holden met my gaze through the rearview mirror. "How was your night last night?"

"Fine." More like completely devastating, but who needed those details?

Lucas turned in his seat as Holden pulled away from the curb. His eyes tracked over my face, pausing on my eyes and cheeks. "You sure?"

I fought the urge to cover my face. "I didn't sleep very well. Are there wild dogs that run in my neighborhood? Something was super loud last night."

Lucas shifted, glancing at Holden.

"Wolves," Holden offered. "There's a pack in the forest. Sometimes they get agitated about something and make a decent amount of noise."

"I thought wolves were endangered."

"They are," Keene said. "But they're making a comeback. The town is protective of the pack here. I think they know that and feel safe."

I leaned back in my seat, looking out my window as if one might pop up right then. "I want to see a wolf."

Lucas cleared his throat. "I bet you will before too long."

No wonder that guy in the woods had warned me about being out there alone. I didn't think wolves were aggressive unless you came between them and their young or their food though. I'd have to do some research.

I hadn't seen the tall, dark stranger at school yesterday, but he'd looked a bit older. Maybe he was in college? There were a couple of different colleges and universities within an hour or so of Cloverdale.

Holden pulled into the parking lot at school, and my stomach dropped. It seemed more crowded than yesterday. Lots of students milling around vehicles and chatting with their friends.

Holden swung into a spot at the front of the lot next to the silver Range Rover I'd seen yesterday. His spot read *Reserved for Holden Pierce, Student Council President*.

"Are all the spots reserved?"

Holden nodded. "Everything's assigned, and kids who have leadership roles, like student council and team captains, get the spots up front."

That made sense. Perks for those who were high-achieving. It only made me more glad that I wasn't one of them.

I unbuckled my seat belt and put on my backpack. When I looked up, I met angry glares. Sadie and her friends were leaning against the Range Rover, but their gazes were fixed firmly on me.

I swallowed and slipped my blank mask firmly into place. I hopped out of the truck, the guys doing the same.

"Rowan, right?" Sadie asked, her voice dripping with disdain.

I simply ignored her. Whatever she had to say, I had no interest in hearing it.

"I asked you a question," she hissed.

"Does someone hear something? Like an annoying fly buzzing around?" I asked Lucas and Keene.

Keene wrapped an arm around my shoulders. "Maybe more like a gnat."

"What the fuck?" Sadie screeched.

Piercing green eyes met mine as we made our way to the front of the vehicles. Anson sent me a grin from where he was talking with two guys and another girl who was pressed up against his side. "Like the spine, new girl."

Something about the low rumble of his tone sent a pleasant shiver over my skin.

Keene pulled me tighter against him as we passed, and Anson's eyes flashed, making that deep green spark. "Stay away from him," Keene whispered.

"Why?" I had no plans on becoming friends with Mr. Womanizer, but I was curious.

Holden fell into step next to us. "He's bad news. Reckless. Always getting into trouble."

"Trust me when I say I have no interest in any of that."

But when I glanced over my shoulder, those green eyes were staring back at me, and something about them made me want to lean closer to the flame.

CHAPTER ELEVEN

T HE SOUND OF A CHAIR SCRAPING AGAINST THE linoleum filled my ears, but I was too focused on the paper in front of me to look up. I studied the way the creek blended into the mossy bank. It wasn't exactly right.

I wanted to capture that hit of peace I'd gotten when I'd found that perfect spot. I wanted to hear the roar of the water when I looked at the drawing. It wasn't there. Not yet. I smudged the waterline with my thumb, melding the moss with the water a little more. That was the thing about oil pastels, you could always change what was on the page.

Someone let out a low whistle. "Impressive."

My head jerked up. Yesterday, the seat next to me at the long table had been empty, but today, those mischievous green eyes looked back at me. "What are you doing here?"

Anson raised a brow. "Getting my art credit for the year. That's not a very warm welcome, Rowan."

"You weren't here yesterday."

A grin spread across his too handsome face. "I'm touched that you were looking for me."

I rolled my eyes. "I just meant that the chair next to me was empty yesterday."

He leaned back in said chair, twirling a pencil between his

fingers. "I transferred." His gaze tracked over my face, down my body. "Visual art suddenly sounded a lot more appealing than theater."

I turned my focus back to my paper and picked up a deep green pastel. I flicked color throughout the water, deepening the creek, making it richer somehow. "Enjoy," I muttered.

"You know, I'm not very good at art. I think I might need a tutor. You could come over after school and—"

"No, thank you."

"Seriously?"

I glanced in his direction, seeing true shock on Anson's face. I had to bite my lip to keep from laughing. "Has a girl never told you no before?"

"In the fourth grade, Lily Kilpatrick broke my heart. Dumped me for Chris Abrams."

I shook my head and traded my green pastel for a brown. I began shaping the forest on the opposite side of the creek. "Did you ever win her back?"

"Nope, she moved to Chicago, I think."

I made a humming noise as I filled in the tree trunks.

"You're seriously good at this."

"I love it." Drawing had been one of the few escapes that had remained after the accident. I could get lost in another world for just a little while. All that would exist was me, the paper, and the universe I was creating.

"It shows."

There was something about Anson's tone, an almost longing in it that had me looking up. "What about you? What do you love?"

The wistfulness disappeared from his expression. "Lacrosse, I guess."

"Team captain?"

He shot me a smug smirk. "Since my sophomore year."

I straightened in my seat, studying his face. "Do you love it or are you just good at it?"

The smirk fell from his lips. "What's the difference?"

"Everything."

I wasn't the best artist. I'd likely never get accepted into a prestigious art program or have drawings in galleries, but I loved it. Something about putting pastel to paper set my soul free. I couldn't imagine not having an outlet like that.

Anson shrugged. "It's good enough for me."

"Okay." I turned back to my drawing.

"So if you don't want to tutor me, how about I take you for a burger after school?"

"I'm not sure your girlfriend would be too happy about that."

"Girlfriend?"

I picked up another shade of green and started in on the pine's bows. "The snarling Sadie."

Anson let out a choked laugh. "Sadie isn't my girlfriend."

"So you let any girl who wanders by sit in your lap?"

"Only the pretty ones."

I made a gagging noise.

"Hey now, don't judge."

I looked up at Anson. That niggling sensation I had about him deepened. A sneaking suspicion that there was more to him than he let on, things that he hid below a carefully practiced façade. "Tell me one real thing about yourself, and I'll go get a burger with you sometime."

Anson's eyes blazed, anger simmering there. That was real, the first authentic thing he'd shown me, even if it hadn't been by choice. "I found out three years ago that my mom cheated on my dad. He's not even my real dad. The guy who's part of my DNA makeup is long gone. None of my friends know. That real enough for you?"

I swallowed, my throat seeming to stick on the action. "I'm sorry—"

"I don't want your pity."

"It's not pity. It's understanding. I'm adopted. Didn't find out until I was eleven. Threw me for a loop. And now…" My words trailed off as my vision blurred, memories of my mom from the night before filling my mind.

"Now, what?" Anson asked quietly.

"Now, I'm pretty sure my parents wish they never would've taken me home."

CHAPTER TWELVE

KIDS LAUGHED AND SHOUTED AS THEY MOVED through the halls, heading for the front doors. I went with the tide, happy to be anonymous amidst the chaos.

Someone shoulder-checked me as they passed. "Watch where you're going, new girl," Sadie hissed.

"Drunk in the middle of the day? Seems like you're the one who can't walk a straight line."

Her eyes narrowed on me. "Stay away from what's mine."

"And that would be?" I asked in a bored tone.

"Anson."

"He was pretty clear that you two aren't an item."

Sadie's face flushed beneath her tanned skin. "We have a complicated history."

"Have fun with that." *Complicated history* was surely code for wanting more than she was getting. I could almost feel bad for her, *almost*. It sucked to want someone who didn't want you back, at least, not in the way that you needed them to. But it didn't give her an excuse to be a raving bitch either.

"Keep. Your. Distance," she growled.

An arm linked through mine, and Cassidy smiled up at Sadie. "Making Rowan feel welcome, I see."

"Keep her with your little band of freaks and away from Anson."

Cass tapped her bottom lip as she tilted her head. "Freaks, huh? That's not what it sounded like you thought when you were trying to get Holden alone in the locker room after gym class."

The red on Sadie's face deepened to the point that it looked as though she might have a stroke. "I don't know what you're talking about."

Cass snorted. "*Sure*. Run along now."

Sadie muttered a few choice words under her breath and headed for the doors.

I slipped my arm from Cassidy's and began to clap. "I bow down."

She chuckled. "She's the worst."

"I'm beginning to see that. She's like a dog with a bone."

"She's always been one of the prettiest girls in school, and she thinks that should give her first pick of all the guys."

I rolled my eyes. "Never mind what any of them want."

"Exactly."

I made my way towards my locker, spinning the dial. "I don't feel too badly for Anson. He brings it on by keeping her around."

Cass leaned against the lockers next to me. "I really don't get that. I know he doesn't actually like her, but he keeps going back for seconds."

Her words had me drifting back to art class, and the pain I knew lived below Anson's carefully crafted mask. "I think it's easier for him to be with someone who doesn't actually know him."

Cassidy's eyes flared for a moment. "You psychic or something?"

I grinned. "Just call me Madame Rowan."

She laughed and then was swept off her feet and tossed over Jack's shoulder.

"I've been looking everywhere for you, Little Bit. You hiding from us?"

Cass pinched his side. "Put me down, Jack."

He did as instructed, slowly lowering her to the floor. As they came face-to-face, he closed the distance, taking her mouth in a long, deep kiss. Cass practically melted into him as Jack's hands slid down her back to her hips. "Missed you today."

"You saw me at lunch."

"Too long."

There was truth in those words, as if Jack could hardly bear to be parted from Cass for a few hours. Something about the tone, the intimacy of the moment, had me looking away, that tugging sensation back in my chest.

I wanted that. The bone-deep knowledge that the person I loved would always be there, no matter what. I certainly hadn't found it with Jason, and part of me wondered if I ever would. Every person in my life who was supposed to love me seemed to find that task impossible.

"Hey."

I hadn't even heard Holden approach and did my best not to jolt. "You're like part jungle cat or something."

His brow arched in question.

"Too damn quiet."

He chuckled. "I'm secretly a ninja."

"Somehow, I wouldn't be surprised."

Holden had that superhero vibe, as if he could save the whole world single-handedly.

He moved in a little closer. "You okay?"

I nodded, shoving a few more books in my pack. "All good." Just lonely as hell.

Holden took the backpack out of my hands before I could put it on. "I've got it." He gave a chin lift to Jack and Cass. "See you guys at home."

"Bye, Rowan," Cass called as Jack pulled her in the other direction.

"See you tomorrow." I closed my locker and spun the dial, following Holden as he started to walk towards the exit. "So you guys all live together?"

Holden glanced down at me, a flash of apprehension flitting across his expression. It was the first time I'd seen him anything less than completely confident and in control. "Not in the same house, but on the same property. I'm sure people have filled your head with all sorts of stuff."

He opened the door for me, and I stepped through.

"I've heard some, but I'd rather hear it from you."

He gave a tight nod as we started towards his truck. "It probably sounds weird from the outside, but for us, it's anything but."

"What is it for you?" I asked.

"It's family. It's having a community always at your back. If one of us is hurting, everyone will do anything in their power to help." The corner of his mouth kicked up. "It's fun too. There's always someone to hang with. Snowball fights and sledding in the winter. Lake parties and epic barbeques in the summer."

"It sounds amazing." The words were out before I could stop them. All I could think about as Holden was describing his life was the empty house I'd be returning to. The mother who couldn't stand the sight of me. The father who didn't bother to come home.

"Really?"

I swallowed against the burn in my throat as I nodded. "Really. I think it would be incredible to grow up surrounded by all of that."

Holden beeped the locks and opened my door for me. "That's not what you had growing up?"

I shook my head. "It was just me and my sister and our parents. Extended family wasn't a big thing." Both sets of grandparents had already passed. My dad had a sister, but we never saw her and I didn't think they were especially close. She hadn't even bothered to come to Lacey's funeral.

Holden shut my door and rounded the vehicle, climbing in. "I can't imagine not having a million people running around at all times."

I wondered if a million people would make me feel less lonely. Or would I simply feel alone in a crowded room? I thought the key was to be surrounded by people who truly knew you, ones who saw and understood. I wasn't sure I'd ever had that from anyone other than Lacey. She saw things about me sometimes even before I did.

Holden started his truck.

"Don't we have to wait for Lucas and Keene?"

Holden shook his head. "They had a meeting and got a ride with Ridge."

Holden's cell phone rang, and he pulled it out of his pocket. "Hey, Dad." While the greeting was casual, Holden's demeanor was anything but. His shoulders pulled tight and his spine stiffened.

"Of course. I'm just taking Rowan home, and then I'll be there." He glanced at the clock on the dash. "Fifteen minutes."

A muscle in his jaw ticked. "I know. I'll hurry." He tapped a button on the screen and dropped the phone into the cupholder.

"If you're late for something, I can walk."

"No, he can wait a few minutes. It's not the end of the world, even though he acts like it."

I was quiet for a moment as Holden backed out of the parking lot. "Tough grader?"

Holden's grip on the wheel tightened. "He expects the best. From himself. From those who work for him."

"From you."

It wasn't a question, but Holden nodded. "Nothing I do is ever quite good enough. He's always looking for the next achievement or learning experience."

"That's a lot to carry."

"I can handle it, but it's exhausting sometimes."

I tried to imagine the opposite of what my current experience was. What if my dad was home every day, asking for test results and wanting to know why I wasn't captain of a sports team? I wasn't sure which was worse, being crushed under pressure or being left completely alone.

Something about the image that came to life in my mind, one of Holden's dad scowling at him in disapproval, had me moving without thought. I reached over and squeezed his leg just below the knee. "Your dad doesn't get to decide what's worthy. He doesn't get to choose your life for you."

Holden's deep blue eyes locked with mine, holding me hostage for a moment. "I wish it was that simple."

CHAPTER THIRTEEN

I WALKED UP THE PATH TO MY HOUSE BUT PAUSED AT THE steps, turning back. I found Holden's stare locked on me, and my heart rattled in my chest. There was so much in that stare, an intensity that pinned me to the spot mixed with what almost looked like yearning, as if it were killing him to pull away.

How bad were things with Holden's dad for him to be this desperate to stay? I lifted my hand. It wasn't a wave exactly, more like an acknowledgment that I saw him. Sometimes simply bearing witness to what someone else was going through was the greatest gift we could give.

Holden lifted his hand too. We both just stayed like that for a few beats, letting all the things unsaid pass between us. Slowly, he lowered his hand and pulled away from the curb.

That tugging sensation in my chest was back, but I forced myself to turn around and walk up the steps. My phone dinged, and I pulled it out of my pocket.

Lucas: *Missed our afternoon joyride. Hope Holden didn't bore you to tears on the way home.*

Me: *Aren't you supposed to be in a meeting? Pay attention.*

Lucas: *So you asked about me, huh? ;-)*

I shook my head and shoved my phone back into my pocket. Unlocking the door, I stepped inside and listened. There were no muted strains of a television show filtering down the hall. My stomach lurched as I set my backpack down. I took two steps towards my parents' bedroom when my mom appeared from the kitchen.

"Where have you been?" Her voice cracked like a whip, and I almost stumbled back.

"At school."

Mom drew her robe tighter around her. "Shouldn't you have been home earlier?"

"We get out at 3:15."

"It's 3:45," she said, as if that proved I was up to no good.

"I had to get my books and wait for my ride. Are you okay?"

She looked freshly showered, yet she hadn't put on real clothes. It was still a pair of pajamas and that bathrobe, but at least they looked clean.

Her eyes narrowed on me. "I'm fine. And I don't appreciate you alluding to your father that I'm otherwise."

The pieces began to fall into place. He must've called, trying to figure out what he needed to do for damage control.

"You didn't leave your room for over a week. You weren't eating. I was worried."

Mom brushed an invisible hair away from her face. "You've always been so dramatic. I'm tired and grieving. I don't need you creating strife with my husband on top of it."

I bit the inside of my cheek. "Okay."

"I ordered takeout. It's in the fridge. I trust you can reheat your dinner without burning the house down?"

I didn't bother answering. I simply nodded.

"I've had a trying day after your father's call. I'm going to rest for a while. Please don't interrupt me. And for God's sake, don't bother him while he's working again. Am I understood?"

"Yes." My voice was void of any emotion. I was systematically turning it all off, piece by piece.

My mother brushed by me, heading for her room.

I started moving. Through the kitchen and out the back door. I was heading towards the forest without really thinking about it. I was deep into the trees before I remembered the warning about wolves, but I couldn't find it in me to care. If they wanted to rip me limb from limb, I just hoped they'd make it quick.

I made my way through the trees. There were a few times I worried I'd made a wrong turn, but then I heard the water. It was soft at first, almost like a white noise machine, but it grew the farther I went. Louder and louder, until it roared in my ears.

I wanted to drown in the sound, to let it wash over me and erase the past ten minutes. I pulled air into my lungs, the scent easing something in me. As the raging creek came into view, a little more of the anxiety and hurt slipped away.

I moved closer to the water and almost stumbled back when ice-blue eyes met mine.

"I thought I told you not to wander around these woods."

My jaw worked back and forth. "And I thought I told you I don't listen to strangers."

He returned his focus to the water as he leaned back against the tree. "Sometimes the warnings from strangers are the best gifts you'll ever get."

"Maybe you could make them silent warnings."

The corner of his mouth quirked up the barest amount, making the scar on his lip stand out. "Fair enough."

I gave Mr. Dark and Brooding his space, picking a spot by another tree. I lowered myself to the ground and leaned against the rough bark of the tall pine. I pressed my hands into the moss at my sides. It was grounding, as if I could simply let the earth swallow me whole.

"Why this spot?" he asked.

I watched as the blue and green swirled, capped in white. "Feels like you could drown out anything here."

He looked my way. "And what are you drowning out?"

I met those piercing eyes, unable to look away. Something in me wanted to tell him. To lay my burdens at the foot of this stranger. "My sister died and my parents are assholes."

His lush mouth thinned. "Succinct."

"What about you? What are you drowning out?"

He turned back to the water. "Ghosts."

His expression went stony as he watched the colors swirl. I wanted to know more, to ask a million different things about what haunted him. But I wouldn't want to answer those questions myself. So instead, I turned back to the creek.

I lost myself in the sound of the water, the feel of the breeze, the cool moss beneath my hands. I let my mind drift. Every time a memory threatened to take me under, I focused on something I could see, hear, touch, or smell.

And not once did I feel alone. Even though this person was a stranger, even though we didn't speak a word, I was comforted by his presence. Something about the knowledge that I wasn't the only one hurting, the only one trying to make peace with ghosts.

At some point, the sky shifted and the breeze turned chilly. I forced myself to stand. "I should go."

He climbed to his feet as I did.

"Thanks for sitting with me—"

"Vaughn," he answered.

My mysterious stranger had a name. "Vaughn," I echoed, my tongue rolling around the letters. It fit him.

He raised a brow in question.

"Rowan."

He nodded. "Let me make sure you get back. We're losing light, and the last thing I need is a dead girl on my conscience."

I stiffened at his words, all the warmth and comfort I'd felt earlier dropping away in an instant. "It sounds like it would be easier for you if I took a tumble off a cliff on my way home."

He took a step closer. "You have no idea what's easy for me and what isn't."

My heart rattled against my ribs. "Well, let me make this one thing easier." I turned on my heel and fled.

CHAPTER FOURTEEN

I HELD A DIET COKE CAN TO MY EYES AGAIN. APPARENTLY, this was how I'd spend all my mornings in Cloverdale. My eyes weren't puffy from crying this time, but they burned from lack of sleep.

I'd tossed and turned last night, unable to get comfortable. My skin felt too tight for my body, and I'd had the deep need to move. For the first time in my life, I'd wanted to go running.

Instead, I'd pulled out my pastels and begun to draw. I'd filled page after page, not even conscious of what I was creating until ice-blue eyes stared back at me. Vaughn. He was taunting me, even in my subconscious.

I lifted the can from my face and cracked it open. Drinking deep, I prayed for it to clear away some of the brain fog. My bagel popped up in the toaster, and I quickly spread some cream cheese on it. Just as I finished, my phone dinged.

Keene: *Consider this me ringing your doorbell.*

I wrapped my bagel in a paper towel with one hand and typed with the other.

Me: *Lazy.*

Keene: *Rude.*

I slid my phone into my back pocket and slung my backpack over my shoulder. Grabbing my bagel and my Diet Coke, I headed for the door. I paused before I opened it, listening. I didn't hear the television, and I wasn't sure what that meant exactly.

Instead of letting myself sink into worry about my mom, I headed for the truck. Keene hopped out of the back seat and held the door open. He gave an exaggerated bow. "Madame, would you like me to lift you into your chariot?"

I snorted. "I could just use you as a step stool to climb in."

"I like the way she thinks," Lucas called from the front seat.

Keene bent at the waist as if to make himself into a stool. I grabbed him by the back of his shirt and pulled him up. "Quit it, would you?"

He shot me a grin that made his ice-blue eyes sparkle. Something about them reminded me a lot of Vaughn's. I hopped into the truck and Keene followed, Holden starting the engine again as we did.

I glanced over at Keene. "Do you have a brother?"

He stiffened and the vehicle went still. "Why?"

My gaze swept around each face pointed in my direction. The expressions were varied, but none were what I'd call warm. "Uh, I met someone who has eyes that look a lot like yours. You don't see many people with eyes that light a blue."

Keene swallowed, and it was almost as if the motion pained him. "Where did you meet him?"

"Um, in the woods. I needed a break from my house and—"

"And you thought you'd roam around some woods you aren't familiar with?" Holden barked.

Lucas put a hand on Holden's shoulder and squeezed hard. "You sound a lot like Vaughn," I muttered.

Keene's head snapped in my direction. "He spoke to you?"

"Why is that weird?"

Lucas was the one to answer. "Vaughn's been through a

lot. He's not overly warm and doesn't really like other people. Especially if he thinks they're encroaching on his territory."

"It's national forest land," I argued.

Lucas shook his head. "Doesn't matter. I'm guessing it was that ridge by the creek?"

I nodded.

"That's his spot."

"He barely lets me go there," Keene muttered.

"So he is your brother?"

"Yeah, older by two years. He and I live close to the creek."

I noticed Keene didn't say anything about their parents. That absence made my chest clench. I moved without thinking, laying my hand over Keene's and wrapping my fingers around his palm. "Your brother's a character, but he's also kind, in his own way."

I thought about how Vaughn had sat with me in silence, making me feel a little less alone. He might've ended the afternoon on a bristly, rude note, but I had a feeling that had more to do with pushing away the intimacy of the moment.

Keene's thumb moved on top of my hand, sweeping back and forth. The action sent a pleasant shiver up my arm. The sweeping motion turned to circles. "Go easy on him. Vaughn isn't like other people."

I wanted to ask a million other questions, but it wasn't my place. I'd just have to hope that I'd learn the story one day. That Vaughn would trust me enough to share it.

Lucas smiled at me from the front seat, his eyes sweeping over Keene's and my joined hands. "Let's hit the road before we all get tardy slips."

"Shit," Holden muttered as he began driving. "My dad will kill me if I get one the first week."

"He'd have your hide if that happened any week," Lucas said.

Holden grunted something under his breath and pressed a little harder on the accelerator.

We made it to school with time to spare. Students were still milling around. Sadie and her crew were still sticking close to Anson and his friends. As Holden put his truck in park, Keene pulled his hand away from mine.

I'd completely forgotten that we were connected, as if it were the most natural thing in the world. When his hand left mine, I felt cold, and that tugging sensation in my chest was back. I clenched and flexed my fingers.

As we slid from the vehicle, Jasmine appeared at Holden's side. She slid her arm through his. "Missed you at breakfast this morning."

Holden straightened his arm, as if hoping that her hands would slip off. They didn't. "Had stuff to take care of."

Jasmine's hold only tightened. "You know I'm around to help." She looked up at him, lashes fluttering. "*Whatever* you need."

Keene let out a half-cough, half-laugh.

I couldn't move. Anger bubbled up in my chest like I'd never experienced before. I wanted to tear her hands from Holden's arm. Rip them from her body.

An arm circled my shoulders. "He doesn't like her like that. Jasmine is that annoying fly he has to be nice to because her mom works with his dad."

I squeezed my eyes closed. Counting up to ten and then back down, I focused on steadying my breathing. What was wrong with me? I had no rights to Holden. He was barely more than a kind stranger.

That was a lie. He wasn't a stranger anymore. Not after the time we'd spent together the past few days. He was a friend.

Yet that didn't seem accurate either. There was an

71

overwhelming desire in me to claim him. To tell Jasmine and everyone else to back off.

When I opened my eyes, Lucas was staring down at me. "You okay?"

"Yeah," I croaked. "Just a weird morning."

Holden had managed to shake off Jasmine and moved to our little huddle. "Everything all right?"

Keene glared at him. "Just peachy." His gaze cut to Jasmine, as if to punctuate the point.

Only she was glaring daggers at me. Crap. I didn't need someone else on the *I hate Rowan* squad.

"Hey, Picasso. How about today for our date?" Anson shouted from his group.

All of the guys around me froze. Holden turned slowly towards Anson. "What did you just say?"

Those words were definitely a growl.

Anson pushed off his Range Rover. "I'm taking Rowan for a burger." He sent me a wink.

I rolled my eyes. "It's not a date. More like a lost bet."

"She can't today," Keene gritted out. "We have that project for history we need to start on."

The project wasn't due until mid-term, so I wasn't sure we needed to start on it today, but I wasn't going to get in the middle of some weird pissing contest.

"She can't any day," Lucas said under his breath.

I smacked his stomach. "How about tomorrow, Anson?" No one got to control who I was friends with, and I had a feeling Anson needed a friend. A *real* one, not these fake hangers-on he was usually with.

"We have plans tomorrow, Anson," Sadie called.

Anson rolled his eyes. "We do not."

"You said you'd help me move the furniture in my bedroom. I asked you at lunch yesterday."

"I don't know what you said at lunch yesterday. You were yammering on like an annoying woodpecker. I would've said anything to shut you up."

Her mouth snapped closed.

"Anson," I whispered. I didn't care that Sadie was a bitch; no one deserved to be talked to that way.

His gaze cut to me. "What? It's the truth."

I shook my head and started for the front doors. They could all drown in their drama together.

CHAPTER FIFTEEN

I SNUCK INTO ONE OF THE BATHROOM STALLS IN THE locker room, hanging my gym bag on the hook. Plenty of girls changed by their lockers, but I'd seen one too many teen horror movies. There was always a chance some mean girl would take the opportunity to snap a photo. No, thank you.

I changed from my jeans and T-shirt into shorts and a tank. The teacher had told us we were going to play volleyball today. I sent out mental apologies to whichever team I was on. I had some gifts—drawing, languages, listening. Team sports was not one of them.

I always dove for the ball at the wrong time or aimed in the wrong direction. When I was ten and Dad had signed me up for soccer, I'd been so proud when I'd made my first goal. Until I realized it was on our own goalie.

I groaned at the memory as I stuffed my school clothes into the bag. At least gym was only a couple of times a week. Maybe I could hide in the back of the group, and I wouldn't even get called on to play.

Opening the door, I moved to my locker and shoved the gym bag inside. There were only a couple of girls left in the room, and I should've hustled but I still dragged my feet.

"All right, circle up. We've got two courts. I'll be breaking you into four teams. You don't have to be an Olympic athlete to get an A in this class, but I do expect you to try. No lazing about." He eyed a girl who was in Sadie's little crew.

"I had a sprained ankle, Coach," she whined.

"All semester?"

Her face flushed. "My doctor didn't want to risk it."

Coach snorted and proceeded to break us into the groups. I fought a groan when he put me on a team with Anson and Jasmine. They were the only people I knew in the whole class, and I would've chosen any other team but this one.

Anson crossed to me, a wicked smile on his face. He bumped my shoulder with his. "Hey, teammate."

I took a step away. "Hey."

His smile faltered a bit. "What's wrong?"

I met his gaze, not looking away. "I don't appreciate getting dragged into whatever dysfunctional thing you have going on with Sadie. You want to screw every girl you can at this school, fine. I'm not going to be on that list. And I don't need another reason for Sadie to set her sights on me. I just want to get through my senior year with as little drama as possible. Honestly, you two are perfect for each other."

Anson's mouth fell open. "I didn't mean—" He cleared his throat. "I'm sorry, Rowan. I didn't mean to put you in a bad spot. I'll talk to Sadie."

I squeezed my eyes closed, pinching the bridge of my nose. "Please don't tell her to lay off me. That'll just make things worse."

He rubbed a hand over his buzzed head. "I really don't understand girls."

"Try treating them like human beings. You might have better luck."

"Hey." He moved in closer. "I treat you like a human being."

I blew out a breath. "There are moments where I think I see the real Anson, just flashes, but I like him a hell of a lot better than whatever macho Casanova you play at the rest of the time."

His mouth pressed into a thin line. "Noted."

"Be whoever you want, just be real in the process."

Anson stared across the gym, his focus seemingly nowhere in particular. "If you don't show people the real you, it hurts a hell of a lot less when they leave."

His words had a careless tone, but they sent little fissures cracking through my heart. "Anson," I whispered.

Those green eyes glinted, not with mischief this time, but with anger. "I don't need your fucking pity." He turned and joined another boy at the front of the court.

"Making all sorts of friends," Jasmine said with a smirk. "I knew it was only a matter of time before the wool got pulled back."

I ignored her and took a place in the middle line. A whistle blew and the game began. I knocked into the people next to me at least half a dozen times. I managed to hit a few balls, but I missed a lot more.

Jasmine scoffed as I blew past another, catching only air. "You could at least *try*, new girl."

I gritted my teeth and stayed focused on the game. The

other team served again. Unfortunately, they'd realized I was the weak link. The ball came sailing towards me.

I focused on not closing my eyes, but it was instinct when a ball was flying at your face. I clasped my hands together and aimed. The frustration of the day, the conversation with Anson, and Jasmine's steady stream of jabs bubbled below my skin.

The volleyball hit my forearms with a crack, the skin there stinging like a dozen wasps had just attacked. The ball flew into the air, hitting the massively high ceiling and then landing with a smack in the opposite court.

"Holy hell," Coach said as he approached, rubbing the side of his face. "That's out of bounds, but you've got an arm on you, Caldwell. You should think about trying out for the team this winter."

I stared at the ball as it bounced off the court, then at the ceiling. *How had I done that?* The whole game, I'd struggled to get the ball over the net, let alone who-knew-how-many feet in the air.

The other team served again, still aiming straight for me. I braced again. This time, I didn't have a chance to go for the ball. Someone crashed into me from behind, sending me sprawling to the floor.

I landed on my side, my elbow and shoulder taking the brunt of the fall. The force knocked the wind out of me, as if I'd been taken down by a two-hundred-and-fifty-pound linebacker.

"What the hell, Jaz?" Anson barked.

"She screws up every time. I was just trying to get us a point."

Coach blew his whistle. "Get off the court and cool off, Jasmine."

She scowled at me but moved to the bleachers.

Anson's face filled my line of sight, but I was too consumed with trying to get my breath back to truly notice.

"Are you okay? Can you move?"

I blinked a few times, my vision clearing. "Yeah. I'll be fine."

"Let's sit you up, nice and easy." Anson reached out a hand, taking mine.

The moment our hands met, a spark lit, but this one was even stronger than the ones I'd experienced before. It coursed through me like an electrical current. Bright spots danced in front of my vision and then there was nothing at all.

CHAPTER SIXTEEN

THE VOICES SOUNDED FAR AWAY, LIKE THROUGH A tunnel.

"See, she's coming around now. You can calm down and take a breath."

"Rowan? Can you hear me? Are you okay?"

The second voice, I recognized. Anson. A hand slipped into mine, warm and comforting. My eyes fluttered open, light breaking through. I groaned as the room came into focus. "What happened?"

The woman, who I assumed was a nurse, patted my leg. "You had a little fainting spell after your tumble. Did you have breakfast this morning?"

"I, uh, a half a bagel, I think." I might not have even gotten that far. I'd been distracted by the revelation that Vaughn was Keene's brother, and the scene with Anson and Sadie in the parking lot.

The nurse made a tsking sound. "That's not nearly enough for a growing girl. Have some of this juice, and you'll be feeling right as rain again."

She bent to hand me the juice, but Anson positioned himself between us, taking the orange juice from her. The nurse raised a brow and then just shook her head, going back to her desk across from the little exam table.

"Here, want to sit up?"

"Yeah."

Anson's hand tightened around mine, pulling me to a sitting position. The room was a little wobbly for a moment and then everything straightened out.

"How did I get here?"

The nurse snorted. "Your knight in shining armor carried you. I thought he was going to tear the school down if you didn't wake up soon."

"Here, drink some of this." Anson placed the juice in my hand.

"You carried me all the way from the gym?"

He rolled his eyes. "You're not exactly heavy."

"I'm tall." Five-foot-eight wasn't exactly short.

"Not as tall as me."

"You're a giant." Actually, all the guys I'd befriended were taller. Significantly taller than most of the school's population.

"Drink," Anson said sternly.

"Yeah, yeah." I took a sip, and the sweet orange taste exploded on my tongue. I didn't think juice had ever tasted this good.

When I emptied the small bottle, Anson took it from me. "How does your arm feel?"

I lifted and bent it, wincing. "I think I'll have a few bruises, but no broken bones."

"Jasmine is such a bitch."

"Language," the nurse warned.

A muscle in Anson's cheek ticked. "She should've been suspended. At least Coach gave her detention for a week."

I let my head drop. Awesome. Now Jasmine would surely have it out for me even more.

A bell rang and the nurse looked at the clock. "That's lunch. If you feel up for it, why don't you get changed and get something to eat. If you're still feeling unsteady on your feet, I can have Anson go get you something."

There was a part of me that would've liked to stay in the nurse's office all day. Maybe she'd let me stay all year. I could do all my classwork in here and never have to deal with another student. Instead, I pushed to my feet. Better to get it over with now.

Anson held out both hands as if to spot me. My mouth twitched. "I'm not going to pass out on you again."

"Better safe than sorry." He bent, picking up my gym bag. "Here. Coach had Ginger bring it for you."

"Thanks." I went into the bathroom and locked the door behind me. I set the bag on a small table in the corner. As I changed, I realized it was more than just my arm hurting. My entire body ached and my lower back twinged. Tonight called for a long soak in an Epsom salt bath.

Placing my gym clothes back in the bag, I zipped it up and opened the door. Anson was two steps outside the door.

"Everything okay?"

A laugh sputtered out of me. "I didn't lose a limb in battle. I'm fine."

That tic was back in his cheek. "You took a hard fall."

I patted his chest. "Let's go get some food. I think you might be falling into some weird hunger-induced, worry state."

The nurse rose, handing me a small cup. "Two ibuprofen. Take these *after* you've eaten. Come back if anything starts hurting more."

"Thank you. I really appreciate it."

"Any time, dear." She patted my shoulder in a grandmotherly way. "Now, shoo, the both of you. My soap is on."

I giggled and started for the door. Anson took my bag off my shoulder. "I've got this."

"Uh, thanks."

We walked down the empty hallway, everyone else having already made their way to the cafeteria.

"So," he began. "Sit with me at lunch today?"

My mouth opened, closed, and opened again. "I'm not sure that's such a good idea. Sadie and the bitch squad aren't my favorite."

"Then we'll sit at another table."

"I'm sure we could sit with Holden, Lucas, and Keene."

Anson's hold on my bag tightened. "We don't get along all that well."

"Why is that?"

"It's a long story. Lots of history there."

I made a humming sound. I wouldn't push, but I was more than a little curious.

Anson held the door open for me, and I stepped through. It was just like when Holden had walked me to his table. All the conversations seemed to mute as gazes turned towards us.

"Why couldn't you be a raging geek?" I mumbled.

"What?" he asked, humor lacing his tone.

"You have to be some hot shit lacrosse player who everyone is obsessed with. Now people are staring."

His hand pressed into the small of my back, guiding me forward. It should've hurt since the muscles there were throbbing, but instead, the contact seemed to ease the worst of the pain. "Come on, we can sit in the back."

Holden stepped into our path. "Hey, Ro. Everything okay?"

Ro. The same nickname Lacey used to call me. It should've gotten my back up, but instead, it was comforting somehow. "I took a spill in gym class—"

"You mean Jasmine basically tackled you," Anson cut in.

"What?" Holden barked.

"Yeah, your little girlfriend is a real piece of work. And I think you're the reason she has such a hard-on for Rowan."

Holden's jaw worked back and forth. "She's not my girlfriend."

"Could've fooled me." Anson's hand moved from my back, his arm slipping around my shoulders.

Lucas and Keene appeared behind Holden. There was a slight panic in Lucas' eyes. "What's going on?"

Anson pulled me tighter against him, letting out a low growl. "We were just going to our table."

"Oh shit," Keene muttered.

Holden's gaze zeroed in on Anson's arm. "Why don't you guys sit with us?"

The words sounded as if they were painful to say.

"Sure," I answered before Anson could tell Holden to fuck off. "That would be great."

Yup, simply wonderful. I'd just have to stave off World War III over peanut butter and jelly.

CHAPTER SEVENTEEN

ASS' EYES WIDENED TO A COMICAL LEVEL AS WE approached. Ridge shifted so that he was blocking most of her from view as he scowled at Anson, and Jack seemed to push in closer to her other side. I sent her a pleading look. The scowls and grimaces from the rest of the guys at the table told me neither of them would be helpful at keeping the peace.

Cass seemed to get my silent message and beamed. "Hey, Anson. How are you?"

He blinked a few times and then cleared his throat. "Good. You?"

"Same old, same old. Already drowning in homework."

I eased onto one of the benches. "Hey, guys."

I got an array of greetings, as Anson lowered himself to the seat on one side of me and Holden took the other.

Cass' gaze flicked to my arm. "Shit, Rowan. What happened?"

"Jasmine knocked her down in gym. Hit her so hard, she passed out afterwards," Anson answered helpfully.

A hard glint appeared in Keene's eyes, the blue going arctic. "Are you serious?"

Anson nodded, jaw tight. "She's a real bitch."

"It wasn't that bad," I argued.

Anson sent me a look. "I had to catch you when you passed out so you didn't crack your skull. I'd say that's bad."

Lucas leaned forward so that he had a better view of me. "Are you sure you're okay?"

"The nurse checked me out. I'm totally fine. I should've had more for breakfast. That's why I fainted."

Cass scanned the cafeteria. "I was wondering why Jaz wasn't here. She never misses a chance to rub up against Holden."

I stole a glance at Holden, whose cheeks had a bit of a red stain. "Are you guys together?"

His eyes flared as he shook his head. "No. I've never given her any reason to think I was interested either." A muscle in his jaw ticked. "But we grew up together. Her mom and my dad are close. There are a lot of people who thought we'd end up together."

An ache bloomed in my chest at his words. I could see them together. Her dark to his light. They'd make a beautiful couple. And if their families were close...

Holden squeezed my thigh, bringing my focus back to him. "I have no interest in her. None. Please believe that."

A burn lit along my throat. Why did that make me want to cry? My skin began to itch, that too- tight-for-my-body feeling that was becoming familiar. I let my eyes fall closed for a minute, trying to center myself.

"Holden, switch seats with me."

My eyes opened at Lucas' words. Holden glared at his friend. Lucas sent him some unreadable message with his eyes, and Holden stood, giving Lucas room to scoot over. Lucas wrapped an arm around my shoulders and pulled me into him. "You looked like you could use a hug."

I melted into his embrace. I didn't care if the entire cafeteria was watching. This had been the day from hell, and I needed a little comfort. The moment Lucas' warmth began seeping into me, the itchy feeling faded.

"Thank you," I whispered.

As I straightened and opened my eyes, I found the whole table staring at me. Cass and Jack with curiosity. Ridge as though I were a puzzle he was trying to put together. Keene sent me a cat-that-caught-the-canary grin. I could swear Holden stared at me with longing in those deep blue depths.

Anson's eyes were wide as he looked from me to Lucas, then Holden, and Keene. "Are all of you—"

"Anson," Holden clipped out. "Not now."

His jaw hardened, but he nodded.

I leaned my elbows on the table and pinched the bridge of my nose. "For the love of all that's holy, can we *please* turn down the testosterone a notch."

Ridge barked out a laugh. "Good luck with that."

Cass reached across the table and patted my shoulder. "When the boys are being dumb, I just ignore them. Works like a charm every time."

Jack leaned in and kissed her neck. "But we can always get your attention back."

I averted my gaze. Something about the gesture was too intimate.

Keene cleared his throat. "Let's talk about our history project. We need to settle on our topic and divide up the research. Can we meet at your house, Rowan?"

I stiffened. Anson seemed to pick up on my tension and moved in closer so that his body was pressed up against mine.

I did my best to keep my face relaxed. "My mom hasn't been feeling well, so I don't think my place is a good idea."

Lucas put a hand on my knee, his thumb tracing lazy circles around my kneecap. "We could always use the library."

Between the pressure and heat of Anson on one side and Lucas' ministrations on the other, I was about ready to combust.

"You guys could come over to my place." There was a slight hesitation in Anson's words, a tone I'd never heard from him before. Anson was always full of brash confidence.

Keene's eyes widened a fraction. "Uh, are you sure?"

"No one's there other than my housekeeper, and I have food—the library doesn't."

Holden nodded. "He has a point. We could all work on homework together."

Lucas looked down at me. "That work for you?"

"Sure." The word came out more like a squeak. "That'd be great."

A hand snaked over Anson's shoulder. Lavender nail polish covered the fingernails in a way I'd never been able to master. "I can come study too," Sadie purred.

Anson shrugged her hand off. "Sorry, Sadie. Not today."

Did that mean another day the invitation would be open?

"Anson, we have a history project too, you know. We should start on that."

My stomach churned at the thought of Anson and Sadie alone together, at all the times they'd been alone together before.

"Sadie," Anson said in a low voice. "Don't make me do this."

"Are you fucking kidding me?" Sadie's shrill tone cut

through the air. "You don't sit with us at lunch, and now you're inviting her over instead of your real friends?"

Anson's eyes hardened into glinting emeralds. "You think you're my *real* friend? You're the furthest thing from that. You're a user, Sadie. You want my money, the status that comes from being attached to me, but you don't know the first thing about me."

"And she does?" Sadie shrieked.

"All it took was ten minutes, and she knew me better than you ever will."

CHAPTER EIGHTEEN

LUCAS GRABBED MY BACKPACK FROM MY SHOULDER, replacing it with his arm. "You weren't trying to give us the slip, were you?"

That warm buzz of energy that always signaled Lucas' nearness slid over me. I did my best not to sigh with contentment. "Running would be useless, you'd just find me."

He barked out a laugh. "You make us sound like stalkers."

I tilted my head back, raising a brow. "Let's be honest, you guys are a *little* stalkerish."

He pulled me in closer. "But you like us that way."

"You are kind of adorable."

Lucas groaned. "Adorable? The kiss of death."

Keene fell into step beside us. "What's the kiss of death?"

"Being called adorable," Lucas answered.

"Ro called you adorable? You're screwed, man."

Ro. There was that nickname again. And just like with Holden, it warmed something in me to hear it again.

Lucas gave Keene a little shove. "She called us all adorable, so we're all screwed."

I shook my head as Lucas opened one of the doors leading out of the school. "Adorable is a compliment."

"Adorable is a compliment for puppies and babies," Keene argued.

"Exactly," Lucas agreed.

"So you'd rather I call you assholes?"

"It'd be better than adorable," Lucas muttered.

Keene shot me a grin. "I'd prefer ruggedly handsome."

I snorted. "So noted."

As we approached the parking lot, I saw Anson and Holden in a heated discussion. *Crap.* I picked up my pace, raising my voice to cover the space, "Hey, guys."

They turned to face me, both masking the earlier tension with smiles. Anson moved to the passenger side of his Range Rover, opening the door. "Ride with me, Rowan."

I stole a quick glance at Holden, whose smile had turned into a glare. "Sure."

"I'll ride with you too," Keene offered. "Always wanted to check out the Rover."

Anson's smile thinned, but he nodded. We all climbed into our respective vehicles, and Anson backed out of his parking spot. "How was the rest of your day? Did Jasmine give you any more trouble?"

I twisted the end of my bracelet around my finger. "No Jasmine or Sadie run-ins." I hadn't even seen Jasmine at all.

Anson adjusted his grip on the steering wheel as he pulled into traffic. "I'm sorry Sadie set her sights on you because of me. I never thought about…"

"How your bed buddies might inflict hell on Rowan?" Keene offered helpfully from the back seat.

I couldn't help it, the laughter bubbled out of me.

Anson sent Keene a glare. "I didn't know she'd go all psycho on me."

"But you did know she was a bitch. Not sure what that says about your taste, man."

I held up a hand. "All right. I think we've all had lapses in judgment when it comes to romantic partners. Let's just move on."

Two sets of eyes turned to me.

"What kind of lapses in judgment have you had?" Anson asked, his voice a low growl.

I pulled the cord tighter around my finger. "Dating someone who it turns out didn't give a shit about me." I'd given Jason so many firsts, and it burned that those gifts had meant nothing to him at all.

"He's an idiot," Keene muttered.

"More like a fucking moron," Anson echoed.

"You're good for a girl's ego."

Anson pulled off the main road onto a smaller one that read *Private Drive.* "Just speaking the truth."

The Range Rover and the street sign should've been my warnings. But when Anson's house came into view, my jaw actually fell open.

It wasn't a house. It was a mansion. Maybe an estate?

"Holy crap," I whispered.

Keene let out a low whistle. "I forgot what a beast of a place this is."

Anson rubbed the back of his neck with one hand as he navigated the circular drive. "It's just a house."

"Sure," Keene said.

I looked up at the massive stone creation. There had to be at least three stories, maybe four. And the grounds surrounding it were meticulously kept. "It's beautiful."

"Thanks," Anson said as he turned off his SUV.

We all climbed out as Holden and Lucas pulled up behind us. Anson waved us inside. "Let's get some food."

As I stepped inside, I couldn't help but stare. The entryway was massive, with two staircases curving up to the second level. The floors looked like they were polished marble and they went on forever. Large windows everywhere let the afternoon light pour in.

We followed Anson as he wove through the space. "Maxi?" he called.

"In here, doll," a voice answered.

We came to a stop in what could only be described as a chef's kitchen. It was impeccably designed with every gadget and gizmo someone could want.

A woman who looked to be in her early sixties turned around at the sound of our footsteps and her face lit up as she took us in. "Oh, how lovely, you brought friends. I'm Maxine, but you can call me Maxi."

"Hi, Maxi. I'm Rowan."

"Lovely to meet you, dear." Her smile was warm and genuine, and I found myself feeling relieved that at least Anson had her at home.

The rest of the guys introduced themselves as well, and then Maxi was shooing us on. "Go on down to the basement. I'll fix you up some snacks."

Anson wrapped an arm around her shoulders and pressed a kiss to the top of her head. "Thanks, M."

"Get going, you big flirt."

I couldn't hide my chuckle, and Anson sent me a mock glare. We went back out into the hall, and I tugged on Anson's shirt. "Is there a bathroom I can use real quick?"

"Sure. Right there." He pointed to a door on the right side. "The stairs to the basement are just a couple of doors down."

"Thanks." I ducked into the bathroom and shut the door behind me. I needed a minute, just a second to catch my breath and get my rapidly beating heart under control. Something about being near all the guys at the same time had my pulse doing acrobatics.

I ran the water as cold as it would go and then splashed it on my face. I pulled one of the rolled-up hand towels from the stack and patted my skin dry. As I met my gaze in the mirror, my cheeks were flushed, and my eyes were a little glassy. "Get it together, Ro. They're just attractive guys. They're your friends. Nothing more."

I tossed the towel into the basket on the floor—apparently rich people only used towels once before washing them—and headed for the basement. As I started down the carpeted steps, I froze at the sound of Anson's voice.

"Four bond mates? I've only heard of that happening twice in pack history. Are you all sure? Maybe you just thought you felt the pull."

Holden let out a low growl. "Do you really think I'd mistake that? That I don't know what it means, feeling like my chest is being ripped to shreds when I have to be apart from her all night?"

"Dial it back, guys," Lucas interjected. "We're all sure. It means she's powerful."

"And that she needs to be protected," Keene cut in.

"With that much power coursing through her, she'll have all the other packs out to get her," Holden said.

What the hell were they talking about?

CHAPTER NINETEEN

THE STAIRS CREAKED AS I MOVED CLOSER TO THE VOICES. I barely heard the slight groan, but four pairs of eyes swung to me. I gave a little wave. "Hey."

"Hey, Ro," Holden said, forcing a smile. "This basement is sick, right?"

I looked around the space, taking it in for the first time. There was a U-shaped sectional that looked like a cloud big enough for twenty people. It faced a massive TV, and there was a coffee table in the middle. On the other side of the room were a bunch of games. A pinball machine, air hockey table, a ping-pong table.

"Whoa," I muttered.

"Want something to drink? We've got every soda under the sun," Anson offered as he moved to a little kitchenette behind the sectional.

"Diet Coke would be great." The enormity of the room and its contents had distracted me for a moment, but now I focused on the guys in front of me. Holden was uneasy, Lucas looked guilty as hell, and Keene avoided my gaze altogether.

I knew the three of them were a part of a community that was different from how I'd grown up. Maybe there was a simple explanation that tied back to that. Then I heard Holden's voice in my head, "*That I don't know what it means, feeling like my chest is being ripped to shreds when I have to be apart from her all night?*"

I rubbed a spot along my sternum. The same place I'd been feeling the tugging sensation. I gave my head a little shake. I wasn't experiencing pain there.

Anson slipped a can into my hand. "Here you go."

Keene smirked at Anson. "What are we? Chopped liver?"

Anson rolled his eyes. "Get your own damn soda." He hopped over the sofa and landed on its cushions. "Make yourself at home."

I rounded the sectional and found my backpack that Lucas must've brought in. I smiled at him. "Thanks, Luc."

"No problem. Do you want to pick our topic for the project first, or do you have other stuff to do?"

I had homework for at least half of my classes, but I could do that once I was home. "We can pick our topic first."

Keene appeared, bringing sodas for him, Lucas, and Holden. "Any preference on what you want to cover?"

Our history teacher, Mr. Clarke, had told us that we could pick any topic as long as it had to do with someplace in the United States, since the class was AP American History.

I sat down on the couch and practically sank into its pillows. "I was thinking it might be fun to do something local. It'll give me a chance to get to know the area a little better."

"That's a great idea," Lucas said, taking the spot next to me and pulling out a notebook.

"My dad might be able to get you into the town's old records, if you need research materials," Holden offered.

Keene cracked his soda and sat. "Perfect. Mr. Clarke eats up that primary resource stuff."

Anson shifted on the couch. "I talked to Mr. Clarke after school, and he said I could switch to your group, if it's cool with you. I think that might be better for me with all the Sadie stuff." His mouth twisted into a grimace on her name.

The relief that swept through me was dangerous. It meant I was starting to care a little too much about who Anson spent time with. "Works for me."

"Less work with four than three," Keene said.

Lucas waved him over. "Welcome aboard."

Anson scooted closer on the couch. "Thanks."

I glanced at Holden who was opening a textbook and laying it on the coffee table. "Are you sad you're not in class with us now?"

He sent me a smile. "Wouldn't mind sharing a few more classes with you."

"Too bad you're a freaking genius and already took AP two years ago," Keene quipped.

My eyes widened. "Seriously?"

Heat hit Holden's cheeks. "I've got a good memory, that's all."

Lucas leaned into me. "Don't listen to him, he's crazy smart. Puts all of us to shame."

I couldn't help but wonder if that was because Holden liked school or because his father was putting pressure on him to excel.

Our group settled on the founding of Cloverdale as our topic and divided up our research tasks. Once we'd done that, we all settled into the couch and began working on homework. I started with pre-calculus. It was my least favorite of all my classes, and I'd learned long ago that I needed to tackle it when I had the most brain energy.

I worked on problem after problem until it felt as if my eyes would cross. I set my pencil down and stretched, cracking my neck. My gaze swept over the group and I smiled. There was something about being comfortable in the midst of total silence that told me I'd found my people.

My gaze caught on Lucas. His brows pinched as he focused on a science textbook. I tapped his leg with my foot. "You okay?"

"Yeah, just have a rough headache."

"I have some extra ibuprofen that the nurse gave me in my bag. You want some?"

He shook his head. "Those painkillers never help."

"Let me try something." I patted the carpet in front of where I was sitting.

Lucas slid off the couch and made himself comfortable in the spot.

I ran my thumbs along the sides of his spine on his neck. "A lot of times, these headaches come from neck tension."

Lucas let out a little groan and all the guys looked at us. I couldn't help the blush that stained my cheeks. "Let me know if it's too much pressure."

"It's perfect."

I closed my eyes for a moment, focusing on feeling where the tension was located most. I kneaded my thumbs into the muscles. I swore I could feel energy flowing out of Lucas—a sort of angry, swirling heat.

Lucas sucked in a sharp breath and my eyes flew open.

"What? Too much?"

Lucas shifted on the floor so that he could meet my eyes. "My headache's gone."

"That's good, right?"

He nodded slowly. "Usually I can't kick them at all, let alone that quickly." His gaze bored into me, as if he was searching for something I couldn't see.

I waved my fingers. "Must have the magic touch."

"Yeah. You must have."

CHAPTER TWENTY

I STARED UP AT THE CEILING AS THE SUN STREAMED IN through my window. I should've been reveling in the fact that I didn't have to be anywhere right now. Normally, I loved a lazy Saturday. Before Lacey died, they'd been some of my favorite days. Dad would make his famous waffles, and Mom would put on The Beatles. Lacey and I would dance around the house until it was time to stuff ourselves silly.

That familiar pang lit through my chest. I missed it all. Lacey, the family we used to have, those perfect Saturday mornings.

My phone buzzed on my nightstand, and I swiped it up.

Dad: *I can't make it home this weekend. Do you have enough money for essentials?*

I stared at the screen, the back of my eyes burning. I tossed the device on the other side of my bed. He didn't deserve an answer. It wasn't like he actually cared.

My phone buzzed again, and I eyed it. There was no new text from Dad, so I picked it up.

Anson: *What are you up to today?*

My heart gave a little stutter-step at simply seeing his name on my screen.

Me: *Don't really have plans. I need to go to the grocery store and do some homework.*

The guys and I had settled into a routine of sorts. School, over to Anson's for snacks and homework, then someone would drop me off. The house was always dark when I returned. Sometimes there was takeout in the fridge, sometimes there was nothing. Every time I checked on Mom, she'd snap at me, so I'd given up. We were just two ships passing in the night.

Walking through the door of this house, I immediately felt lonely. As if all the comfort of having friends with me all day long disappeared in a flash. I had a feeling weekends would be the worst. I had hours upon hours to kill all by myself.

I felt that tugging sensation along my sternum, almost as if the bones were twisting and trying to come out of my chest. I rubbed the spot, trying to alleviate the feeling.

Anson: *Want a ride to the grocery store?*

Keene had asked me once if I had a driver's license. I'd said yes, but I didn't like to drive. They'd left it at that, but I knew they were curious as to the why of it all.

Me: *That'd be good. What time?*

Anson: *Pick you up in twenty?*

Me: *I'll be ready. Thanks, A.*

I threw my covers back and started for my bathroom. I took the world's fastest shower and then brushed my teeth. Tugging on a T-shirt, I paused, my fingers tracing over the skin on my arm. Two days ago, it had been a deep purple. Today, there wasn't a single sign of a bruise.

I stretched out the limb, then bent it. There was no tenderness with the movement at all. I stared at my arm as if it might give me the answer. Something weird was happening with my body. The tugging sensations in my chest, the times I felt like my skin was too tight for the rest of me, this bizarre, speedy healing.

My phone buzzed on my bed, and I hurried to grab it.

Anson: *Here.*

I shoved aside the thoughts of all the freakish things happening to me and grabbed my purse. I hurried down the stairs and out to Anson's SUV.

As I hopped in, I noticed the dark circles under his eyes. "Are you okay?"

Anson took my hand in his, linking our fingers. His whole body seemed to sigh at the contact. "Better now."

My skin hummed at the contact, my palm heating as it lay against his. Anson wasn't shy about touching me but holding my hand felt different somehow, more intimate. He gave my hand a squeeze and then released it. I missed the buzz of energy, the warmth, as soon as it was gone.

"Let's get you some groceries."

"Yeah. Thanks for driving me."

He glanced over at me as he pulled away from the curb. "Be honest. Would you have texted one of us to ask for a ride?"

I bit my bottom lip. "The store isn't a bad walk."

"Ro," he groaned. "We all have cars. We want to help if you need it."

"I don't *need* help. I could've gotten groceries on my own."

"I know you could, but you shouldn't have to. We want to make life easier for you."

"Why?" It was the question I'd been dying to ask since the guys had befriended me. I could see now just how many people, girls and guys alike, wanted to be let into their circle. Why was I the one they'd welcomed?

Anson met my eyes through the rearview mirror. "Isn't that what friends do? Good ones, anyway?"

"I guess." It felt like more though. As if there were some

piece of the puzzle I was missing that the rest of them could see as clear as day.

"Sounds like you haven't had very good friends in your life before."

Anson might've had a point with that one. I hadn't gotten a single phone call or email from my friends back home since I'd moved to Washington.

"What about you? Have you had good friends?"

His jaw worked back and forth. "I used to, and I think I will again."

Holden and Anson were natural-born opposites, made to butt heads and disagree. But it seemed like they were both trying.

I reached over and squeezed his leg. "You've got me."

His gaze met mine for a brief moment, but in those few seconds, so much passed through his eyes. "I do, don't I?"

"And you better be careful because you're stuck with me for life."

Anson chuckled. "I think I can live with that."

I hoped he could because the idea of losing him, losing any of them, made it hard for me to breathe.

CHAPTER TWENTY-ONE

A KNOCK SOUNDED ON MY BEDROOM DOOR, MAKING me jump. It opened before I had a chance to say *come in*. My mom appeared in my doorway, pulling her robe tighter around herself. Her eyes were a little glassy, almost unfocused. "Why haven't you been texting your father back?"

I swiveled my desk chair so I was facing her. "He texted to say he wasn't going to be home this weekend. I didn't think it merited a response."

Her jaw hardened. "It's disrespectful not to return a message."

I wanted to laugh. Disrespectful? Were we really concerned with appearances now? Mom never left the house except to refill the prescriptions that lined her nightstand. Dad wasn't even bothering to pretend he lived here anymore. Did it really matter if I returned Dad's text?

"I'll keep that in mind." I turned back to my homework.

Mom gripped my chair and swung me back towards her. "You will do more than that. You'll text him back right now and tell him you're fine."

The pieces started to come together. Dad had called her to check on me, and she was mad about the hassle.

"Fine." I picked up my phone and typed out a text.

"Happy?"

"You're an ungrateful, little brat. I didn't want to adopt, but your father just had to have another child. We should've taken it as a sign when I couldn't get pregnant and left it at one."

I sucked in a sharp breath. Her words stung like a million, tiny paper cuts. For the past six months, I'd done everything I could to hold on to my empathy for my mother, but I couldn't keep my grip on it any longer. The only option was to shut down every feeling when it came to her, this woman who used to be warm hugs and kind understanding. Now, she was a stranger.

"Okay," I said, voice flat.

"Okay?"

"I don't know what else you want me to say. I'm your greatest mistake. I ruin everything. Okay. I can't change your mind. I'm doing my best to stay out of your hair. You only have to deal with me for one more year. Then I'll be gone. You won't ever have to see me again."

That truth cut, deeper than the nicks of her earlier words. What I knew as fact now carved itself into my bones. I pictured shutting off every avenue of care I had about my parents. It was the only way I'd make it through.

She blinked a few times. "Fine. But I'll be keeping an eye on you. Your father doesn't need any more stress worrying about you, and neither do I."

She turned on her heel and left, slamming the door in her wake.

I slowly turned back to my desk. My hand trembled as I picked up my pen. I tried to focus on the words in my Spanish textbook, but they blurred. After a few more tries, I gave up, pushing to my feet and circling the room.

The tugging sensation in my chest was back, only it was worse, more painful. My phone dinged.

Lucas: *Hey, haven't heard from you today. Everything okay?*

My fingers hovered above the keyboard as my chest ached. I wanted to tell him that I was as far from okay as you could get. I wanted to ask him to drive to my house, just so I could have a hug. So that I could assure myself there were people in this world who cared about me. Then I thought about how my mom had turned into a completely different person on a dime.

Me: *Just been busy. Have a lot of homework.*

Three dots appeared on my screen, then disappeared, and finally appeared again.

Lucas: *I'm here if you need anything.*

A tear slipped free, splashing onto my screen. I wanted to lean into that, to reach out, but I couldn't make myself take that leap.

I turned the phone on silent and put it in the drawer of my nightstand. I didn't want to see any other messages, it didn't matter who they were from. Instead, I pulled back the covers and crawled into bed. Switching off the light, I prayed for sleep.

It didn't find me quickly, and once I slipped under, it was fitful. Full of tossing and turning and endless dreams.

I was running through the forest behind my house. I couldn't see it, but I knew something was chasing me, some sort of shapeless, dark force I knew would drag me under if it caught me. Branches slapped at my face and stung my arms.

The night closed in around me, making it hard to see. I tripped over a tree root, the skin on my knee tearing as I fell. I scrambled to my feet and pushed my muscles harder. My lungs burned as I heard something gaining on me from behind.

I skidded to a halt as I reached the embankment of the creek, heart hammering in my chest. Howls pierced the air. My gaze jumped to the source of the sound.

Wolves. Five of them, pacing on the other side of the creek. I stumbled back a step. The black one with a white patch on his chest growled at my retreat. I froze.

Thrashing sounded in the woods behind me.

All the wolves growled now. The loudest sound came from an almost golden wolf. His muscles tensed, and he leapt across the ravine. I braced for attack, but the wolf didn't even pause, taking off past me towards the sound.

The rest of the wolves followed him. All but one. His coat was a mix of colors: blonds, grays, and reds. His hazel eyes seemed to see right through me.

He approached slowly, head low. I couldn't pull air into my lungs. The wolf sniffed the air and then lowered to almost a belly crawl.

He nosed my side, his head seeking contact, nuzzling. He made a soft keening noise as he moved. I reached my hand out slowly, lowering it to his head. The wolf pressed against it, almost encouraging me to pet him.

My mouth curved as my heart hammered. "You want a head scratch?"

Another howl pierced the air, and the wolf leapt to his feet, growling. The move sent me tumbling back.

I woke with a gasp, clutching at my chest. My hand tingled. I swore I could still feel the soft fur against my palm. I flexed and clenched my fingers, trying to make sense of the sensation. It had been so real.

I threw back the covers, taking a few steadying breaths and trying to get my heart under control. "Just a dream."

I listened for a moment. I didn't hear a thing. I rose from the bed and grabbed a sweatshirt from my closet.

I needed fresh air. My room was too stuffy and stale. I padded down the stairs and through the kitchen, towards the back deck. I paused for a moment before I opened the door, staring at the woods that had felt so real in my dream.

"Don't be stupid." I forced myself to open the door.

The cold night air hit me like a wall of calming weight. I pulled in a lungful, and it soothed the worst of the panic.

Moving towards one of the Adirondack chairs, I pulled on my sweatshirt. I eased into the chair and tugged my knees up to my chest. With all that had happened over the past week, it was no surprise I was having nightmares. My mind was simply melding the stress with the warning I'd gotten about the wolves. Only something in my brain had turned the wolves into protectors instead of predators.

I liked thinking of them that way. I'd need to do a little research, see what wolves actually looked like. In my dream, they'd been massive and majestic. I wished I could call them back now, then maybe I wouldn't feel quite so alone.

Movement in the trees caught my eye. I strained to see what it might be. Shadows shifted, and I lifted my sweatshirt hood over my head as I shivered. Just the wind making the trees sway. Then a howl lit the air.

CHAPTER TWENTY-TWO

I GROANED AS I ROLLED OVER. I RAISED A HAND TO COVER my eyes from the sun streaming in through the window. Deep sleep hadn't found me again all night, and I knew I'd pay for it today. At least it wasn't a school day.

I pulled my phone out of my nightstand. An array of text messages dotted the screen, but I couldn't take them in, not when the date screamed out at me. I'd known it was coming. Yet, there was some part of me that wanted to shove the reminder to the back of my brain.

Lacey had always complained about her birthday being in September. *"Everyone's cranky that they're back in school. No one wants to celebrate."*

I'd always gone out of my way to make sure she felt loved each year. She'd always slept like she was in a coma, so I'd sneak into her room at night and decorate it. One year, I'd filled it with so many balloons, she could barely find the door.

I curled into a ball. God, I missed her so much. She wouldn't even recognize the family she'd left behind now.

That tightness took over my body, the urge to move. I jumped out of bed and moved to my closet, pulling on workout gear. I quickly brushed my teeth and then headed downstairs. I didn't pause to listen for Mom or let myself wonder if she was okay, I simply kept right on moving.

My steps faltered for the briefest of moments as I crossed into the forest. My dream was still fresh in my mind. I could still see the eyes of those wolves glowing in the dark.

Instead of letting any fear or what-ifs take hold, I started to jog. Pushing my muscles into a run helped. The burn and strain took away some of the itchiness I felt, even if it did nothing for the ache in my chest.

By the time I reached the creek, my chest was heaving, and I had to bend over to try to catch my breath. The air hurt as I sucked it in, but I welcomed that bite of pain. Any distraction.

I let myself crumple to the bank, my muscles cramping. My finger twisted around the tails of the bracelets on my wrist, Lacey's and mine. There should've always only been one there.

The tears started, spilling over and down my cheeks, coming as fast as the water below. Sobs racked my chest, but they were silent ones, as if it hurt too much to give voice to the anguish living inside me.

"Ro?"

My head snapped up as a figure stepped through the trees. In the sun-dappled landscape, it took me a moment to tell whether it was Vaughn or Keene, but the soft concern lining Keene's face was the giveaway.

"Hey," I croaked.

He moved so fast, I swore my vision blurred. In a flash, I was scooped up and deposited onto Keene's lap. He cradled me against his chest. "What happened?"

I hiccupped, trying to get more air into my lungs. I didn't know what to say. How to put all I was feeling into words. I went with the simple truth. "It's my sister's birthday."

"Ro." Keene skated a hand over my hair and down my back, pulling me even closer. "I'm so sorry. First one, right?"

I nodded into his broad chest.

"The firsts are the hardest. It's never easy, but it's not always a sucker-punch to the gut."

I lifted my head, taking in Keene's face, his eyes full of so much understanding. "Who?"

His jaw tightened, and I thought he might not answer. "My parents. There was an…attack on our compound. Some angry, sick people. A lot of us lost someone. Holden lost his mom too."

"I'm so sorry. I hate even saying that because it's such a cop-out, not nearly enough, but it's all I have."

His fingers linked with mine. "There are no good words when it comes to grief. It's being present and listening that matters. I'd like to be that for you. Do you want to tell me about her?"

My throat constricted, but I felt a pull in me. I wanted to share Lacey with someone else. I didn't want to hide her away in dark corners, afraid of how my parents would react. I slid off Keene's lap but kept hold of his hand. The simple touch was grounding, as if it were the only thing tethering me to the earth at the moment.

"Lacey was obsessed with space."

Keene's brows rose. "Space?"

"Ever since she was little. She always said she'd be an astronaut one day. She'd beg our parents to order her astronaut ice cream so she'd be *ready* for her mission. As she got older, that turned into astrology, and she thought the stars could tell us about our lives."

"They are a force much greater than ours."

My mouth curved. "Lacey would always say something similar. She was the best big sister." My voice caught on the words.

"She was driving me home from a concert when we got in the accident. My parents wouldn't let me go alone, so she took me. If I hadn't been so determined to go—"

"No." Keene released my hand and wrapped his arm around my shoulders, pulling me tight against him. "It was an accident. You can't blame yourself."

"My mom does."

"I'm sure she doesn't—"

"She told me flat out."

Keene sucked in a sharp breath. "Grief can twist some people up."

"I know. Doesn't mean it doesn't kill, but I know she's wrecked. And the fact that my dad never even bothers to come home anymore doesn't help."

"I think things like this either bring people together or drive them apart."

I tipped my face back to take Keene in. "Did it make you and Vaughn closer?"

He was quiet for a moment, staring at the water. "In some ways, it did. In others…things aren't easy for him, and he doesn't appreciate it if I try to help."

"He's your big brother. I'm sure he thinks it's his job to look out for you."

"We should look out for each other."

I leaned deeper into Keene's side. "That is how it should be."

A twig snapped, and Keene was instantly on his feet. The set of his shoulders relaxed just before Vaughn stepped through the trees.

I swallowed hard as Vaughn's arctic gaze cut to us. "You should walk her home. I found fresh tracks on the other side of the creek."

"What kind of tracks?" I asked as I pushed to my feet.

"Wolf."

My heart gave a little stutter in my chest. "I had the craziest dream about wolves last night."

Keene turned, alarm passing over his expression. "What happened in the dream?"

"It's not a big deal. Just a nightmare. I was running through the woods, to this spot actually. Someone or something was chasing me, and then there were these five wolves. They protected me, I think. They chased off whatever it was."

Keene moved in closer. "Did you say five?"

"Yeah."

"You're sure?"

"I'm sure. Why does it matter?"

Keene glanced at Vaughn, who was staring right at me. "Five can be a symbolic number in dreams."

"Oh." I fought the urge to squirm, and Vaughn's gaze pinned me to the spot.

"Vaughn's right. I should get you back."

"Don't come out here alone, Rowan," Vaughn growled low.

His voice had a tremor to it, one that skated over my skin and sent a pleasant shiver up my spine.

"Wolves don't want anything to do with me."

He scoffed. "Don't be an idiot. They'll take whatever hot, juicy meal they can find."

CHAPTER TWENTY-THREE

MY PHONE BUZZED AS I TOOK THE LAST SIP OF MY Diet Coke.

Lucas: *Hurry your cute butt up.*

Anson and Holden had begun taking turns with who picked me up each morning. While they were getting along better, we hadn't yet progressed to all five of us piling into a single vehicle yet.

I tossed my can into the recycling and picked up my backpack. As I opened the front door, I paused. There was a small package on the porch. I bent, picking it up.

My name was scrawled across a small, white card.

Rowan,

Put this under your pillow. It will guard your dreams.

There was no name at the bottom, but it had to be from Keene. I unwrapped the paper and pulled out a pinkish crystal with some sort of leather cording around it. The stone was beautiful, and I swore I could almost feel a warmth seeping from it.

Keene waved to me from the truck. I quickly wrapped the crystal in the paper again and started towards the vehicle. Keene jumped out of the back seat and held the door for me.

I picked up my pace. "Why didn't you text me when you dropped this off last night?"

"When I dropped what off?"

I unwrapped the stone, showing it to him. "This is from you, isn't it? The card said it would guard my dreams."

Keene took the crystal from me, studying it. Something passed over his face—a cross between worry and relief. "It's from Vaughn."

"What?"

Vaughn didn't exactly come off as the warm-and-fuzzy, leaves-presents-on-your-doorstep type. Yet, he'd gone out of his way to make me feel safe while I slept.

Keene cleared his throat and handed the charm back to me. "We have a friend who makes these. He must've asked her to do a sleep one for you."

I stared down at the pink stone, rubbing my thumb over the surface. "Will you tell him thank you for me?"

"You can tell him yourself." He took my phone from my other hand and began typing. "He's in your phone now."

We climbed into the truck, but I couldn't look away from the name on my screen.

"What was all that about?" Holden asked.

Keene buckled his seat belt, not looking in Holden's direction. "Vaughn left Rowan a dream charm."

Holden's gaze jumped to me. "Really?"

"I guess so."

Lucas made a sort of humming noise in the back of his throat. "You're good for him, Ro."

"I don't know about that. He mostly scowls at me."

Holden chuckled. "Trust me, from Vaughn, that might as well be a hug."

My fingers moved slowly across my screen.

Me: *Thank you for my charm. It's beautiful.*

A few seconds later, my phone dinged.

Vaughn: *Don't just stare at it. Use it.*

Me: *Bossy even in text message.*

He didn't respond, but I knew he was somewhere, scowling at his phone.

———⚜———

I slid onto the cafeteria bench between Lucas and Anson, and bumped both their shoulders with mine.

Anson pushed in closer, the heat from his body sinking into mine. "How was astronomy?"

"Good. I need to do some stargazing this weekend, which should be fun."

He leaned in, his lips almost grazing the shell of my ear. "I'll stargaze with you this weekend."

A roll hit Anson square on the chest, and Keene sent him a look. "We can *all* look at stars this weekend."

"Yeah, yeah," Anson grumbled, settling back in his seat.

As I gained a few inches of distance, my lungs reinflated. I swore my hormones were going haywire. Every time one of the guys touched me, my nerve endings felt as if they were catching fire, burning me from the inside out.

Lucas' hand landed on my knee. "Morning was okay?"

I automatically did a scan of the cafeteria, my gaze landing on Sadie, who was cuddled up with one of Anson's supposed friends. She glared at me.

"It was fine."

There had been a few snide "slut" comments tossed around by Sadie and her friends, but she'd gotten smarter about it. She no longer said or did anything in front of Anson, Holden, Lucas, or Keene.

"Good," he said and offered me a chip from his bag.

I took it and popped it in my mouth. "Thanks."

"Ro, any other plans this weekend?" Holden asked.

"I don't think so."

"We're having a barbeque at the compound, you should come."

"Are you serious?" Jasmine asked. "That's a horrible idea."

"Shut it, Jaz. It's not your place to decide that kind of thing," Cass cut in.

Jack wrapped an arm around her shoulders as Ridge glared at Jaz. "She has a point."

Jasmine's amber eyes darkened. "It's more my place than any of yours."

I stayed quiet as the back-and-forth played out.

"Enough," Holden barked, turning to Jaz. "You're already on thin ice. Don't make it any thinner."

Her grip on her fork tightened, but she lowered her gaze.

Holden turned his attention back to me. "So, can you come? Saturday afternoon."

I focused on unwrapping my sandwich. "I don't want to make anyone uncomfortable."

"Then try sitting somewhere else for lunch," Jasmine muttered.

Cass brought her elbow down on the edge of Jasmine's lunch tray, tipping it into her lap and sending food everywhere. "Oops."

"You fucking bitch!" Jasmine yelled as she jumped up, brushing salad off of herself.

Ridge was on his feet in a flash, backing her up. "Watch your language."

Jasmine threw up her hands. "You're all crazy. Ever since *she* showed up. She's not the second coming." With that, she turned on her heel and stormed out of the cafeteria.

Cass bent to pick up the salad pieces from the floor. "I should feel bad about that, but I just can't."

I grinned at her. "I'd say, worth it."

Keene shook his head. "You two together are trouble."

"Just remember that," Cass quipped.

Holden stared after Jaz. "I don't know what's gotten into her lately."

Anson snorted. "Seriously? You have no idea?"

Holden sent Anson a withering look. "You know what I mean."

I shifted in my seat, and Lucas wrapped his hand around my leg. The worst of my apprehension seemed to almost melt away at his touch. "I'm sorry I've made things complicated between you two."

Holden's gaze snapped to me. "There is no *us two*. She's a childhood friend, that's it."

"Sure, but I'm messing with that."

Lucas squeezed my leg. "Jaz needs to make peace with the fact that she and Holden will never be together. The sooner that happens, the better for all of us."

"Please come on Saturday," Holden said.

The plea in his tone had my reservations crumbling. "Okay. What should I bring?"

Holden beamed. "Just yourself."

"It'll be fun," Cass assured me. "You'll get to know everyone in our little pack."

I hoped she was right. But if Jaz was in charge of the welcome committee, I'd likely get a knife to the back.

CHAPTER TWENTY-FOUR

I SURVEYED MY APPEARANCE IN THE MIRROR FOR THE eighty-third time. The jeans were my favorite pair, the ones that made me seem like I had more curves than I actually did. I paired them with a short-sleeved, maroon blouse that deepened the color of my auburn hair. I'd dusted on a little eye shadow and a coat of mascara. After some lip gloss, I was ready to go.

My stomach gave a healthy flip. I'd be meeting the guys' whole community. The nerves that bubbled to life were a mix of being unsure of what to expect and fear that I wouldn't be accepted into their close-knit group.

I stared at my computer. The temptation to do some digging about the secretive group had been niggling me all morning. Then I'd remember how it felt to have my hardest moments exposed without my permission. As desperately as I wanted more information, I couldn't bring myself to do it.

My phone buzzed on my desk, and I hurried to pick it up.

Holden: *I'm here.*

Me: *Be right out.*

I stuffed my phone into my purse and headed downstairs.

"Where do you think you're going?"

I skidded to a stop in the entryway, turning to face my

mother in her familiar robe. Her eyes were red and glassy, and she was leaning against the wall.

"I'm going to a barbeque at a friend's house." I didn't bother using Holden's name. She didn't know who any of my friends were. "Do you want me to make you something to eat before I go?"

Mom's eyes narrowed on me. "I can make my own breakfast. Did your father give you permission to go to this barbeque?"

"Yes." I'd never made a habit of lying to my parents. I hadn't needed to. While they'd been protective, they'd never been unreasonable. But now...it felt like there was no other option. I doubted she'd check with Dad.

"Fine, but you need to be back by seven. I'm sure you haven't done all your homework."

"Okay."

My mom turned, unsteady on her feet. She nearly crashed into a wall but caught herself at the last second. I bit the inside of my cheek as she disappeared into the kitchen, picturing all the pill bottles that lined her nightstand. My stomach churned.

Instead of following her, I stepped outside, locking the door behind me. I gave a *one minute* signal to Holden, and he nodded. I pulled my phone out of my bag and hit the contact for my dad. It rang five times before clicking over to voice mail.

"Hey, Dad. It's Rowan. Um, I'm going to a barbeque at the Pierces', and I told Mom you said it was okay. I, uh, I'm worried about her. She seemed a little out of it this morning, and she's taking a lot of prescriptions. Maybe you could come home tomorrow and check on her? Make sure everything's under control? Thanks."

I paused for a moment. I wanted to tell him I loved him but couldn't get the words out. We'd always been a family who threw love around like confetti. Now, the sentiment felt awkward and unpracticed.

I hit end and slid the phone back into my bag.

Holden's gaze tracked over my face as I rounded the truck and climbed in. "Is everything okay?"

I pulled the seat belt across my lap and buckled it. "Yeah."

"Ro."

I bit my lip to keep the tears at bay. "My mom's a mess. I'm worried she's taking too many meds, but it's not like I can ask her, she'd only bite my head off."

Holden was quiet for a moment, but he slid his hand into mine, linking our fingers. "Does your dad know?"

"He's never home, so he doesn't see it. I just left him a message and asked him to come check on her."

"That's good. I could have my dad call him too—"

I shook my head, cutting Holden off. "I don't think either of them would handle it well if they knew I was talking about her to other people."

"I get that, but this stuff is serious. People can accidentally overdose pretty easily."

I twisted the end of my bracelets around my finger. "I know. I think I'll try to sneak in there tonight and take pictures of all the meds. I'll call her doctors if I have to."

"That's not a bad idea. She may be using different doctors to get multiple prescriptions."

The bitterness that rose up in me was strong and swift. I hated myself for it. Anger at my mom, that she could find the energy to get herself to multiple doctors, to the pharmacy, but she couldn't find it in herself to ask me one kind question, to hug me, anything.

Holden tugged my hand so that I leaned into him, and curled

his other hand under my hair, around the back of my neck. He pressed his lips to my hair. "You're not alone. You know that, right?"

Did I? There was a comfort I felt when I was with one of the guys or all of them that I'd never known before. Not even when Lacey was alive and our family was whole. But as beautiful as that comfort was, I couldn't seem to hold onto it. As if it were sand, slipping through my fingers.

"Thank you," I whispered.

Holden squeezed the back of my neck. "You'll learn to trust it over time, to trust us. We want to be there for you."

I straightened, searching Holden's eyes. Those deep blue pools held truth and something more. Something I wasn't quite ready for.

Heat pooled low in my belly as I swallowed. Holden's lips were just a breath away. So close that, if I just leaned forward, I would know what they felt like, what they tasted like.

"I want to be there for you too, you know. This isn't a one-way street."

Holden's mouth curved, my gaze tracking the movement. "You are. Just being with you…I feel peace. I haven't felt that in a long time."

I thought about what Keene had said about Holden's mom being killed in the attack. "I'm here if you ever want to talk about anything. We could have a code word."

He chuckled. "What should our code word be?"

"Pink, fluffy bunnies?"

Holden shook his head as he released his hold on my neck and started his truck. "I need something more manly than that."

I tapped my lips in an exaggerated thinking gesture. "Meat, potatoes, and monster trucks? That's manly, right?"

Holden's lips twitched. "How about sea glass?"

"Sea glass?"

"It's what your eyes remind me of. They're green, but in certain lights, they can almost look blue. Just like how sea glass is in the sun."

My throat caught as I struggled to swallow against the burn. People rarely noticed that my eyes did that, changed color in certain lights. They usually didn't care enough to pay that close of attention. But Holden had.

"Sea glass. I like it."

His gaze caught mine, and he linked our fingers again. "I do, too."

CHAPTER TWENTY-FIVE

HOLDEN GUIDED HIS TRUCK ALONG A GRAVEL ROAD, leading us farther and farther from town.

"How long does it take you to get to my house?"

He maneuvered to avoid a dip in the road. "Only like ten minutes."

"It feels like a whole other world out here."

The forest seemed to arch around us, creating a tunnel around the road. The lush trees and foliage were so thick, I couldn't see more than a few feet in any direction.

"It's a different feel, for sure." Holden pulled to a stop at a large, wooden gate.

I leaned forward in my seat as he rolled down his window. There were cameras pointed at the vehicle and also the surrounding fence line. Holden pressed his thumb to a pad, and the gate buzzed, slowly opening.

I let out a low whistle. "That's pretty high-tech."

"We don't scrimp on safety. Keene helped put it all together, actually."

"Our Keene?"

Holden guided his truck up the drive, the gate closing behind us. "The one and only. He's great with all things security and tech.

But if you get him started talking about it, he'll never stop and he'll probably put an alarm system on your locker."

I chuckled. "I'll keep that in mind."

We drove for a few more minutes, the forest opening up a little more, giving me a chance to see through the trees. Cabins of various sizes appeared here and there.

"So your dad owns all of this?"

Holden shifted in his seat. "More or less. The community owns it, but he's in charge of the community."

"Like a president?"

"Kind of."

"Do people have to pay rent?" I asked. I couldn't quite understand how it all worked.

Holden shook his head. "It's a true community. Everyone has a job that helps us be self-sufficient."

"Like a commune?"

Holden's lips twitched. "Just call us wannabe hippies."

It wasn't such a bad idea. I would've loved to have help with my mom, someone to go to so that I could share my concerns. Instead, everything had landed on my shoulders, and I was buckling under the weight.

The trees parted, giving me a peek at another cabin. I let out a small gasp. Cabin was the wrong word. This was more like a mountain mansion. The structure itself almost faded into the woods surrounding it, as if it had sprung from the land itself—a combination of rough wood and smooth stone, with a black, metal roof.

"It's beautiful."

Holden pulled to a stop beside the building. "It's big, but it's where we have all our meals and meetings."

"No one lives here?"

"Dad and I do. Coby and Jasmine, too."

I stiffened. "You and Jasmine live together?"

Holden rubbed the back of his neck. "Not like that. She and her mom have rooms on the opposite side of the house."

My stomach twisted, nausea sweeping through me. I could only imagine how often Jasmine found herself at Holden's door.

Holden reached over and grabbed my hand. "I have no interest in Jasmine. Less than zero."

"Okay." I hated how soft my voice sounded. What right did I have to wonder if Holden might be interested in Jaz? I was drawn to more than just Holden. Even the idea of having to choose made me physically ill. I couldn't imagine a life without any of them, even prickly-pear Vaughn.

"Ro?"

"Sorry. I'm a little all over the place. That's all."

He nodded slowly, still keeping hold of my hand. "You know, it's okay if you have feelings for more than one of us."

"What?" My voice went all high-pitched on the question.

Holden's mouth curved. "It's okay if you're feeling a pull in multiple directions. That isn't weird or abnormal here. It's fairly common. I just wanted you to know that."

My heart hammered against my ribs. "O-okay." What else could I say? I couldn't begin to imagine how that would work. I tugged my hand from his. "We should go."

"You're right."

I climbed out of the truck, and by the time I was down, Holden was waiting for me. He inclined his head towards the side of the lodge. "Everyone should be around back."

I nodded as his hand found the small of my back, guiding me forward. Voices lifted on the air, punctuated by shrieks. As we rounded the building, a crowd came into view. There had to be three or four dozen people milling about—kids running in circles, playing some sort of tag game, and adults in various groups. And a spread of food that looked like it could feed an army.

"Wow," I mumbled.

"We go big on barbeque days."

"I can see that."

Slowly, all the eyes of the crowd shifted towards us, and I found myself inching closer to Holden instinctively. "Why are they staring?"

Holden swept his thumb back and forth across my back. "We don't get a lot of new people around here. Give them a few minutes, and they'll all forget that you're new."

I did my best to hold on to that promise.

The crowd seemed to almost part as Holden's father made his way towards us. His smile was warm, but his sheer size was intimidating—he had an almost lethal energy to the way he walked. "Rowan, I'm so glad you could make it."

He extended a hand to me, and I took it. "Thank you for having me, Mr. Pierce."

"Please, call me Mason. We aren't formal around here."

"Okay."

"Let's introduce you around." His gaze cut to Holden. "Come with us."

It wasn't a question, but Holden dipped his head in agreement.

He led us to a small group in the center of everyone. "Rowan, these are my right hands, Coby and Sam."

I would've known that Coby and Jasmine were related without even hearing her name. She was taller than Jasmine, but she had the same dark hair and amber eyes. And those eyes were currently fixed on me. She swept her gaze up and down, and then raised her chin, as if finding me lacking.

The man next to her was almost as tall and broad as Mason, but not quite. He shook his head at Coby. "Take a chill pill, Cobes." He grinned at me. "It's nice to meet you, Rowan. Holden and the guys have told me a lot about you."

My cheeks heated, but I accepted the hand he offered. "It's nice to meet you too. You work with Mr. Pierce? I mean, Mason."

Coby snorted and Mason glared at her, shutting Coby right up.

"More or less. He runs the ship around here, but I make sure it runs smoothly," Sam said.

"Sounds like an important job."

"It is," Mason agreed.

A wave of whispers swept through the crowd, making me look around.

"Well, I'll be damned," Sam muttered. "He came to a barbeque."

My gaze followed Sam's and locked with ice-blue eyes. They froze me in place. I couldn't move, even if I'd tried. Vaughn was here.

CHAPTER TWENTY-SIX

VAUGHN'S GAZE SWEPT OVER THE CROWD, AND I SAW the wince, the flicker of unease, in his eyes. I was moving before I could think about it, weaving through the crowd until I reached him. I came to a stop just one step away, unsure of what to do now that I was actually here.

"Hey." *Hey? Seriously, Rowan?* That was the best that I could come up with?

Vaughn's eyes tracked over my face, as if he were committing each feature to memory. "How have you been sleeping?"

"Better. No more scary dreams."

"Good."

I shifted on my feet. "You're here."

Vaughn grimaced as he took in all the eyes focused on us. "I'm regretting that decision."

"Vaughn." Keene looked back and forth between us as he walked up with Lucas and Anson in tow.

Vaughn lifted his chin in greeting but didn't say anything. His gaze held on Anson for a few beats, assessing. Anson met his stare dead-on, not looking away.

I sent Lucas a pleading look. He was the one who was always the best at breaking tension.

He cleared his throat. "Why don't we go get some food? Or we could give Rowan a tour of the compound?"

"Oh, no," Cassidy called as she walked up. "You guys always keep Rowan to yourselves. I promised our girl that I'd give her a tour. You guys can go help with the grilling."

Keene opened his mouth to argue, but Cass sent him a withering stare. He sighed. "Thirty minutes. If you don't bring her back by then, we're coming to find you."

"I'll need over an hour if I want to show her all the good stuff," Cass argued.

"Forty-five minutes," Keene countered.

"Oh, fine." Cass linked her arm with mine and tugged me away. "Let's go before one of them follows, thinking they're being stealthy."

I choked on a laugh. "A forty-five-minute rule does seem a little ridiculous."

Cass shrugged and led me away from the lodge. "They're a little territorial with all the guys around."

I bit the inside of my cheek to keep from asking what she meant by that. I wasn't sure I was ready for the answer. Things were changing so fast, I felt like I could barely hold on.

"So, you saw the lodge. That's one of the main hangouts. But the lounge over here is the other. There are games and a massive TV. There's another one for the younger kids too, with practically a whole fun zone of stuff."

"Wow." I wasn't sure what else to say.

Cassidy's steps slowed as she turned to me. "You okay?"

"There's just been a lot lately."

She gave me a kind smile and reached out to squeeze my arm. "I can only imagine. Just remember, you only have to put one foot in front of the other. And you can ask me anything you want. I'm an open book."

I fought the urge to squirm. "With Ridge, Jack, and Cooper, how does that work?"

Cass grinned. "It's easier than you think. There's a period of adjustment while you're working out the kinks, and it takes open and honest communication, but now it's as easy as breathing. I couldn't imagine not having each of them. They balance me."

"But why would they want to share one girl?"

Cass put a hand on her hip. "Rowan Caldwell. Are you doubting my ability to charm three guys into falling in love with me?"

My cheeks heated. "No, I just—"

"I'm kidding. It's normal for us. There are more men than women here. And we believe that some of those bonds are destined." She met my gaze. "Are you really going to tell me that you haven't felt a pull towards some of those guys at our lunch table?"

I liked the idea of having partners who were destined for me. Like somehow, we would make each other the best versions of ourselves. But I wasn't sure how realistic that was. "Couldn't it just be hormones and chemistry?"

"That certainly plays a role, but it's more than that. You'll see."

Jasmine stepped out from the trees by the lounge. "She won't see. Because she doesn't belong here. And Rowan knows that. Don't you?"

I didn't let Jasmine's words hit, refusing to give her that kind of power. Instead, I rolled my eyes, leaning towards Cass. "She's pretty dramatic, huh?"

Cass giggled. "Her one-woman shows are epic."

"Laugh it up all you want, but I saw how everyone treated you when you walked in. Like a pariah. You'll always be an outsider, never trusted to truly be one of us. And Holden needs someone who is woven into this community. He's going to be our next leader, and he can't do that with you by his side."

Little embers of doubt pricked at my skin. So much of what Jaz said, I had no idea about. Holden hadn't once mentioned taking over for his father one day. And I couldn't help but wonder if he hadn't shared that with me because I wasn't a part of his world.

Jaz's mouth curved. "I see you putting together the pieces. The sooner you do, the better it'll be."

"Back off, Jaz. You're so twisted up over Holden, you can't even recognize lies when they spill out of your mouth anymore. Get it through your thick skull, he doesn't want you."

Jasmine's hands curled into fists at her sides, and her breathing became almost labored. "Don't forget who the dominant is around here, Cass."

Cass straightened, stepping in front of me. "Don't forget who can kick your ass in hand-to-hand."

"I won't stop with hand-to-hand. You don't get to say that shit and get away with it. Holden's been mine from the day I was born. Everyone knows it."

"Everyone but him, maybe," Cass shot back.

"He needs time," Jaz gritted out.

"I don't need time." Holden appeared from seemingly out of nowhere. "This ends now, Jaz. If you don't back off, I'll take disciplinary action."

"Holden." Her voice was the softest I'd ever heard it. "You

can't mean that. We've been through everything together. I know you better than anyone."

"That's not true. Not anymore."

His fingers linked with mine. There was a buzz of energy and heat with the contact.

Jasmine zeroed in on our joined hands, her gaze practically burning a hole through them. "You'll regret this."

Her words were a vow, and I had no doubt she'd do everything in her power to bring them to fruition.

CHAPTER TWENTY-SEVEN

HOLDEN TURNED TO ME AS JAZ STORMED OFF. "I'M SO sorry, Ro."

Cass cleared her throat. "I'm going to give you guys a minute. But don't let her get in your head, Rowan. She's just jealous."

I rubbed the beads of my bracelet between my fingers, staring at the rose gold catching the sunlight.

Holden placed a knuckle under my chin and lifted my head to face him. "Cass is right. Jasmine's jealous and isn't used to feeling that emotion."

"I don't understand your relationship with her." It was a request for an explanation, one I didn't have rights to but was asking for anyway.

Holden's hand fell away as his gaze drifted to the forest. "It's complicated."

"Okay…"

A muscle in his jaw ticked. "There's a lot I can't explain, not yet, but Jaz and I both have a lot of pressure on our shoulders to achieve certain things. When we were younger, she was who I went to when I needed to vent."

The flare of jealousy hit me square in the chest, stealing my breath. "What changed?"

"Jaz did. I don't know when it happened, but instead of being on my side, it felt like she was just another source of pressure."

"Her mom and your dad want you guys to be together?"

Holden toed a rock with his boot. "Her mom does. My dad did, but I don't think he'll want that for long."

"Why won't he want it anymore?"

"There's a lot that's changed over the past few weeks, but I need time to tell him. I don't want—" Holden shook his head, cutting himself off. His eyes met mine. "I know I keep saying I'll explain everything, I just—"

"Need time," I finished for him. "It hurts. You know so much about me, and it feels like you're hiding a whole other life."

Holden winced. "I'm sorry—"

I held up a hand. "I don't want an apology. I just wanted to explain where I'm at. You can't ask me to open up to you when you're not willing to do the same."

He nodded slowly. "You're right. Do you want me to take you home? Or are you all right with staying?"

I let out a shuddering breath. Part of me wanted to retreat to my room, to my solitude, but it wouldn't solve anything. If I wanted to know the guys better, I needed to know their world. "Let's go back to the barbeque. I'm hungry."

Holden's mouth curved, but the smile didn't reach his eyes. "Well, we've got plenty of food."

He didn't touch me while we walked, seeming to know I couldn't handle that right now. Voices grew louder as we approached the group. Sam threw a boy, who looked to be around nine, high into the air. The little boy shrieked as he was caught and then squirmed out of Sam's hold and took off. He collided with me with an *oomph*.

I caught his shoulders with a laugh. "Whoa there."

He blinked up at me, eyes wide. "You're really pretty."

Holden chuckled. "You know how to win them over, Crispin."

"You're the new girl, right?" he asked as he studied me.

"I am. Think you could show me the ropes?" I offered a hand, and Crispin took it immediately.

"I know all the best spots for hide-and-seek."

Sam hurried over to us. "Sorry about that."

I smiled reassuringly. "No problem at all. Crispin was just going to show me around since I'm the new kid on the block."

Sam glanced at Holden, as if checking to see if that was okay, and Holden gave a nod of assent. "Just let me know if he gets to be a bother." Sam ruffled his son's hair. "Best behavior, okay? Rowan is our guest."

Crispin puffed out his chest. "I'm her tour guide."

"Okay then." Sam sent me a grateful smile as Crispin led me towards a bean-bag toss game.

Lucas appeared at our side, his hand going to my free one. "You okay?"

"Better now."

He grinned at me. "That's what I like to hear." He looked down at Crispin. "Got a new friend?"

Crispin nodded. "I'm going to show her how to play the toss game."

Holden moved in closer, his gaze searching mine. "Will you be okay here for a little while? I need to talk to my dad."

"Sure. Do whatever you need to."

A flicker of hurt passed over Holden's eyes, and guilt pricked at my stomach.

"Okay. I'll be back soon."

Lucas watched as Holden walked away. "You going to tell me what happened?"

"Later," I muttered. "So, Crispin, how many people are on each team?"

"Two."

I scanned the people around us, my eyes falling on Keene, Anson, and Vaughn talking on the outskirts of the crowd. "I'll get our fourth." I walked over, and without giving myself a chance to think about the wisdom of my actions, took Vaughn's hand. "Crispin is teaching me the toss game. You're on my team. Anson and Keene, you can cheer us on."

Keene's jaw fell open as he looked at Vaughn's and my joined hands. "All right then…"

I kept moving, tugging Vaughn behind me. He finally shook his hand free from mine, scowling at me. "You're bossy, you know that?"

"I guess I learned from the best," I said with a pointed stare.

He shook his head.

Crispin's eyes widened as he took in my teammate. "Are you sure you want Vaughn?"

I chuckled, looking over at the man in question. "I see your reputation precedes you."

Vaughn's scowl only deepened. "Let's just play already."

Crispin explained the game, and we began to play. Before long, we were in a spirited, round-robin tournament with a whole lot of smack talk. I couldn't remember the last time I'd laughed this hard. We drank and ate as we rotated in and out of different teams. I got to meet some of the guys' friends and extended family members. But Crispin was my favorite.

He gave me a high five. "We are awesome!"

"That we are."

"Crispin," Sam called as he approached. "It's time for us to head home."

"Aw, Dad. I don't wanna."

Sam pinned him with what I could only call a dad stare.

Crispin's shoulders slumped. "All right." He threw his arms around me in a tight hug. "You'll come back, right?"

"Promise. We have to keep practicing if we're going to kick Vaughn's butt."

I looked up at Vaughn, expecting to see another scowl, but instead, his expression was unbelievably gentle as he took in Crispin and me. That look had something going funny in my stomach.

Crispin squeezed harder and then let me go. "See you soon."

"Thanks again," Sam said.

"Anytime."

Vaughn moved in closer as Crispin and Sam walked away. "You're good with him. He needs that."

I looked at Vaughn. "He didn't mention his mom at all…"

Vaughn's jaw clenched. "She was killed."

A wave of pain and nausea swept through me. "Poor Crispin."

Vaughn didn't say a word, simply stared off into the woods.

My phone buzzed in my pocket, and I pulled it out.

Mom: *Where are you?*

I took in the time. 7:30. Crap.

Me: *I'm so sorry. I lost track of time. Coming home now.*

There was no response. Double crap.

"Can someone take me home? I'm late and my mom's pissed."

Anson tossed his bean bag at the other hole. "I've got you."

"Thanks." I looked for Holden and his father to thank them but didn't see them anywhere. "Lucas, can you tell Mason thank you for me?"

"You got it, Ro."

I hurried with Anson to his SUV and climbed inside. I knew I'd have hell to pay with my mom, but even knowing that, there was a warmth flowing through me that I hadn't felt since Lacey had passed. It was a feeling of family, I realized. I just hoped this one was stronger than my last.

CHAPTER TWENTY-EIGHT

I LEANED BACK IN MY SEAT AS ANSON GUIDED HIS RANGE Rover down the mountain roads. "How was today for you?" I hadn't been the greatest friend to him today. Too focused on the Jasmine drama, and then I'd gotten swept up in the fun of the afternoon.

Anson tapped out a beat on his steering wheel. "You know, it shocked the hell out of me, but I actually had fun."

I choked on my laugh. "You really didn't like Holden, Lucas, and Keene, did you?"

Anson's tapping slowed. "It's complicated."

I twisted in my seat so that I could fully see him. "Can you tell me why?"

Anson opened his mouth and then closed it again. "I can't yet."

"What is it with you guys telling me there are things I need to know, but you can't tell me yet? It's freaking infuriating."

His eyes widened a fraction. "It's not that we don't want to, but…"

"But what?"

"Holden's dad has to give the okay."

I froze. "Seriously?"

Anson nodded. "There's a lot you don't know."

"I'm aware, but you aren't a part of Mason's community."

A muscle in his cheek ticked. "My sperm donor was."

"What?" The word came out in a hushed whisper. "Anson, was he there today?"

"No, he's long gone. But he tied me to them, and that's complicated for me."

Understatement of the century. "Do they want you to come live there or something?"

"They'd like me to, but for now, they aren't putting too much pressure on me."

I laid a hand above Anson's knee. "You don't have to do anything you don't want to. You know that, right?"

"It's—"

"Complicated. I know, but they don't get to dictate your life."

Anson's lips twitched. "You gonna take them on for me?"

"Hey, I took a self-defense class once. I can kick some serious ass if I want to."

"I'll remember that."

"Good."

Anson pulled to a stop in front of my house.

"Are you going to be okay by yourself tonight?"

He reached up and tucked a strand of hair behind my ear. "I'm used to being alone, Ro."

I threw my arms around him, burrowing into his chest. "I don't want you to be alone."

Anson's fingers tangled in my hair. "It's not like it used to be. I don't feel lonely. You changed that."

My breathing hitched as I pulled back, our faces so close now. I wanted to close the distance, to know what it would be like to drown in those lips. The light over my front door flashed on, and I jolted. "I better go."

139

"Text me later, and let me know how it goes with your mom?"

"Sure." I climbed out of the Rover and jogged up the front steps. I tried the door, and it was unlocked. As I stepped inside, a voice called out from the kitchen.

"Come in here now, Rowan."

My stomach dropped at my mom's hard tone, but I forced myself to move in the direction of her voice. "I'm really sorry, I completely lost track of time and—"

My voice cut off as I rounded the corner and took in my mother's face. Rage was the only word to describe it. Hot fury burning through her eyes. "You're grounded. School and home for one month. That's it."

Her words slurred a bit around the edges, and I took in the tall glass of clear liquid in front of her at the kitchen table.

"Mom—"

"Don't call me that," she hissed. "I'm not your mother. I'm the woman who's stuck with you for another year."

I swallowed down the burn that flamed to life at her words.

She pushed to her feet, legs trembling slightly as she did. "You will no longer bother my husband while he is working. I see what you're doing, trying to create problems for us, to drive a wedge in there, but it won't work."

"I was worried about you—"

"Shut up!" she screamed. "My life is none of your business. If you don't want to be cast out on the street when you turn eighteen, you'll do what you're told and not create any more problems for me."

My temper lit at her accusation. "You're the one creating the problems. Popping pills and drinking yourself under the table. I was trying to help because I was worried about you!" Except it wasn't her that I was worried about. It was the mother I used to know. The one who no longer existed. I wanted her back so badly it felt like claws digging into my heart. "This would break Lacey's heart if she could see you right now."

"Don't you say my daughter's name!" Mom picked up her glass and hurled it at me.

It happened in slow motion. The heavy, crystal cylinder hurtling towards my head. I tried to move, to duck, but the shock was too strong. The glass hit the wall next to my head, shattering. Shards splintered, and I cried out as several sliced my skin. My hand flew to my face.

Mom stood there, blinking rapidly, as if she couldn't believe what she'd just done. "Go to your room."

The alcohol from the glass burned my cuts, as I held my hand to my face. I didn't wait for any other orders, I ran for the stairs. My whole body trembled as I slammed the door to my room. I shoved my desk in front of the door, not willing to risk her coming back for another piece of me.

Once it was in place, I stepped back. Blood smeared the surface of the desk, and my shaking intensified. My phone began ringing in my purse. I ignored it, letting the purse fall from my shoulder, and moved to the bathroom.

I froze as I took in my reflection. Three slices across my cheek were oozing blood that tracked down my neck, to beneath my shirt. A sob tore free from my chest.

My phone started ringing again.

I picked up a washcloth as more sobs came, running cold water over the cloth. I cried out as I pressed the fabric to my cheek. But after the worst of the sting faded, the coolness of the water was a balm to my cuts.

The ringing stopped, then started up again. I just kept staring at my reflection in the mirror. My face had no color, only making the streaks of blood on my neck stand out more. My eyes were huge. Shock. My brain knew I was in shock, but that knowledge didn't make my appearance any less startling.

A tap sounded on my window and I jolted, letting out a small shriek. My heart hammered against my ribs as I stepped out of the bathroom. Lucas' face appeared in my window, and he motioned for me to open the pane.

God, I didn't want to. If I did, there would be questions, ones I wasn't ready to answer. Yet, if I didn't, I knew he wouldn't go away.

I moved to the window seat, unlocking the window, and began to open it. Lucas pushed it the rest of the way, hoisting himself inside. "Rowan—" His sentence cut off as he took me in. I knew what he was seeing, and none of it was good. "What happened?"

The growl to his words had me falling back a step. Lucas didn't growl, he wasn't intimidating. He was my gentle giant.

He closed his eyes for a moment, as if trying to get himself under control. When he opened them again, his expression was gentler, though still a touch feral. "Rowan. What happened?"

"I, uh, uh—"

"The truth. Don't come up with some lie."

That was exactly what I'd been searching for. Some believable story. That I'd tripped and clocked myself in the face. That I'd been attacked by a rabid cat. Something. Anything but the truth.

"My mom." My voice caught on the words. "She threw a glass at my head."

Lucas' hazel eyes darkened to a color I'd never seen in the natural world. "I'll kill her."

CHAPTER TWENTY-NINE

LUCAS WAS MOVING TOWARDS THE DOOR, BUT I STEPPED into his path. "Luc, stop."

"She. Hurt. You," he gritted out as his chest heaved.

"I'll be fine. And you can't confront her—she'll only be angrier that you're here. I'm supposed to be grounded."

"I don't care what you're supposed to be. She can't get away with this."

"She's drunk, Luc," I whispered. "She probably doesn't even remember what she did."

His jaw tensed, and then he rolled his shoulders back. "Let me see your cheek."

"It's not that bad."

"Let me see it, Ro. I have to see if we need to take you to a doctor."

I slowly lowered the washcloth as he moved in closer.

"Fuck. This is bad. You might need stitches." He bent and picked up my purse, riffling through it and pulling out my phone.

"What are you doing?"

He put it to his ear. "Calling Holden." He paused for a moment. "Yeah, I need you to come get us. We need to go to your dad—"

"No!" I gripped Lucas' arm. "Not Mason."

"Hell," he muttered and then turned his attention back to the call. "Just come get us. We'll meet you out front." He hung up and tossed the phone into my bag.

"I can't leave with you. If my mom finds out—"

"It sounds like your mom is two seconds away from passing out, and if you think I'm just going to leave you here, you have another thing coming."

I closed my eyes but felt Lucas' heat as he moved in even closer. He carefully pressed the cloth back to my cheek as his other hand cupped the unmarred side of my face. "I need you to let me take care of you right now. Please."

It was the sheer devastation in his tone that did it. I opened my eyes to take in the hazel ones before me and nodded.

"Let's go." He grabbed my purse and backpack, and then slid the desk away from the door. A muscle in his cheek ticked as he took in the bloody fingerprints.

I gripped his arm as he opened the door. We stood there for a moment, listening. I didn't hear anything, and Lucas motioned me forward.

We crept down the stairs. Each time a plank groaned, I winced and prepared myself for my mother's screams. They never came. Lucas slowly opened the door, flipping the lock on the handle once I'd stepped through.

Headlights appeared as we descended my front steps, but Lucas stayed close, a hand on the small of my back. He opened the door to the cab of Holden's truck, and I climbed inside.

"What the hell is going on?" Holden asked, turning in his seat. He sucked in a sharp breath as he took in my face.

"Luc?" Keene asked from the front seat.

"Her fucking mom."

I swore the temperature in the truck went up twenty degrees, but maybe it was just the fire in the eyes staring back at me. "Please stop," I whispered.

Lucas moved in closer, wrapping an arm around me. "Sorry, Ro. We're not mad at you."

"I know that, but—"

"It's too much. I know. Just lean on me."

I burrowed into Lucas' body, pressing my unmarred cheek to his chest. "Thank you."

"If she doesn't want to go to my dad, where are we going?"

"Anson," I said softly. "We're going to Anson's."

Holden pulled away from the curb while Keene called Anson. The soft tones of the conversation swept over me, but I didn't even try to discern the words. I didn't care. I wanted to float away into nothingness.

I let myself do just that, lulled by the beating of Lucas' heart. Before long, Holden was pulling to a stop, and my door flew open. Anson pulled me gently out of the truck and into his arms.

"Baby, no." His voice was ravaged.

"I'm okay," I croaked.

"You're not," he bit out. "But you will be." He carried me through the open door and into the kitchen, setting me on the counter. "We need to clean those cuts."

"Okay."

An engine sounded at the front of the house and then raised voices. Anson moved to stand in front of me as Vaughn tore into the kitchen.

"Move," Vaughn growled.

"After you take a breath," Anson shot back.

"I need to see her."

I placed a hand on Anson's shoulder. "It's okay."

"You sure about that, Ro?"

"I'm sure."

Anson moved aside but only the barest amount. Vaughn stepped forward, his hands flexing and clenching. "Why didn't you tell us this was happening?"

"It hasn't happened before. Not like this."

"Swear it," he growled.

"I swear." I reached out to take his hand, but Vaughn stepped out of my reach. "Don't."

I snatched my hand back. "Sorry."

"I have to go. I need to run." Vaughn spoke to no one and everyone.

Keene gave him a jerky nod. "We'll be here."

And with that, Vaughn was gone.

It was just one more hurt, but I couldn't take it. I shut down. I could hear the conversation around me, but I wasn't truly taking it in.

"I need to call Doc," Holden said.

"She doesn't want that kind of attention," Lucas argued.

"Look at her face," Holden shot back.

Anson pulled a kit out of one of his cabinets. "I can fix it."

Everyone in the room turned to him.

"What do you mean?" Keene asked.

He began pulling out gauze, tape, antiseptic, and a small tube of something. "I got in my share of fights after my dad bailed. I can fix this."

Lucas took a step forward. "Are you sure, man?"

"You think I'd touch her if I wasn't?" he barked back.

Holden put a hand on Lucas' shoulder. "Let him treat her. He knows what he's doing."

Anson nodded at Holden and walked over to the sink to

wash his hands. "It'll go better if I have one person helping me. Someone with steady hands."

"Me," Keene said and moved to the sink to wash his hands as well.

They patted their hands dry with paper towels and then came back to me. Anson stood directly in front of me. "The first part is the worst. It's going to sting."

"Okay." I couldn't find it in myself to care. It couldn't hurt worse than the rest of the night.

Anson poured some antiseptic onto a gauze pad and pressed it gently to the cuts on my face. I didn't move. My eyes burned, but I didn't let the tears fall.

"Almost done with this part. Just need to make sure the cuts are clean." After a few more swipes, he threw the gauze in the trash. "Keene?"

"Yeah?"

"I need you to hold the cut together while I glue it."

"Glue it?" Lucas snapped. "Are you crazy?"

"He's not," Holden defended. "They use a form of superglue in hospitals every day."

Anson uncapped a tube. "Got my own medical-grade shit right here."

"Handy," Lucas muttered.

Keene moved in, raising his hands to my face. "I'm so sorry if I hurt you."

"It's okay," I whispered.

He and Anson moved in tandem over my cuts, sealing them closed. I wasn't sure how long it took them, but eventually, they both stepped back.

Anson scanned my face and then moved back to the kit,

pulling out a bottle of pills. He shook two free and grabbed a glass of water. "Take these."

I did as I was told. "Can I shower? I-I need to get clean."

The desperate need clawed at my insides. As if the blood staining my skin would cement the pain and anguish there too.

The feeling was mirrored in Anson's eyes. "We'll get you clean."

CHAPTER THIRTY

I MOVED THROUGH THE HOUSE LIKE A ROBOT. ANSON'S HAND didn't leave the small of my back as he guided me up the stairs and down a hallway. He opened a set of double doors and ushered me inside.

As I inhaled, a sense of home washed over me. The familiar comfort of Anson, of knowing I was safe. The burn in my eyes picked up again.

"The bathroom's through here," Anson said as he moved across the large space.

I could feel the rest of the guys following behind us. Their collective heat almost reaching out. Still, I shivered.

Lucas moved forward, wrapping an arm around me. "Cold?"

I nodded.

"A shower will help," Holden said. He looked at Anson. "Do we need to cover the glue so it doesn't get wet?"

"Yeah. But after twenty-four hours, it's fine." He pulled a bandage out of his pocket and motioned me into the bathroom. "We can take this off after you're done with your shower."

I didn't say a word, simply stepped forward and tilted my head to give Anson better access to my cheek. His large hands were remarkably gentle as he carefully smoothed the bandage over my face. Then he bent and pulled out a set of towels. "These are clean. I'll get you a T-shirt and sweats that you can sleep in."

"Thank you." My voice was barely above a whisper, but I couldn't seem to get it any louder.

He stepped out of the bathroom, and Holden stepped forward. His hand ghosted over my unmarred cheek. "You'll be okay. You're so damn strong."

I knew I would be okay, that I'd made it through worse and I would make it through this too. But sometimes I didn't want to have to be strong. Right now, I wanted to fall apart. To sink into that dark abyss I felt hovering below me.

Anson wove his way around Keene and Lucas, setting a pile of clothes on the counter. "They'll be big on you, but the sweats have a drawstring." He cleared his throat. "Do you need help?"

Keene's eyes flared. "I think she can handle this part on her own."

"I've got it," I cut in before an argument could start. "Thank you."

The guys slowly filed out of the bathroom, closing the door behind them. Their muted voices filtered through the door, but I shut the sound out. I didn't want to hear their concern or pity. I didn't want to hear anything at all. I moved to the shower large enough to fit twenty and turned the water to hot.

Slowly, I peeled off my clothes, leaving them in a pile on the floor. My muscles screamed with each movement. Only my face was truly injured, yet it felt as if I'd been hit everywhere.

I opened the door to the shower and stepped inside. The hot water scalded my skin, but I welcomed it, letting it pour over my face and down my body. I watched it swirl around the drain, streaked with red.

The red of the blood washed away. Yet, somehow, I knew it

would always stain my skin. The world wouldn't see it running down my face, caking my neck, but I would. Evidence of my mother's hatred.

A sob tore free as I dropped to the floor. I pulled my knees to my chest and held them tight, rocking back and forth. The woman who had loved and cared for me almost all my life now despised me with everything she had in her.

Tears streamed down my face, mixing with the water of the shower. I couldn't hold it in anymore. The pain. The grief. The loss of what once was.

Sobs rocked my body with a violence I'd never experienced before. I struggled to suck in air, my lungs refusing to obey my commands.

A knock sounded on the door. "Rowan? Are you okay?" Lucas asked.

I couldn't get any words out as I sputtered and wheezed.

"Ro?" His voice was more urgent now.

My fingers began to tingle and dark spots danced across my vision, but my sobs didn't stop. It felt as if I was having a heart attack. Maybe this was the end. I'd cease to be from a broken heart.

The door opened a crack, but I couldn't make anything out through the steamed glass. I heard a muttered curse, and then the door to the shower swung open. I couldn't find it in me to worry about my nakedness.

"Ro." Lucas' voice cracked as he sank to the tiled floor. He pulled me into his lap and wrapped his arms around me.

"What the hell is going on?" Holden barked.

"Turn off the water and get me a towel," Lucas shot back.

Holden did as instructed, shutting off the shower and wrapping a towel around me as I struggled to breathe.

Lucas put one hand on my non-injured cheek and the other

on my neck, letting out a grunt as he did. "Let it go. You have to release it, Ro. It'll kill you if you don't."

"I-I-I can't." I struggled to get the words out.

"Give it to me. I can take it." He pressed his lips to my temple. "Close your eyes and release."

My eyes shut, as if listening to him and not me. I could feel the pull of something in my chest, a phantom energy. Instead of fighting it, I gave myself over to it. I released my hold on all the pain and let it fly.

Then everything went black.

CHAPTER THIRTY-ONE

I WAS WARM. ALMOST TOO WARM, BUT ALL I WANTED TO DO was burrow deeper into the heat. I felt safe. Cocooned. As if nothing could hurt me, as long as I stayed exactly where I was.

My eyes fluttered open, a soft light filling my vision. Slowly, my surroundings came into focus. A large, vaguely familiar bedroom. Anson's room.

The night before came back to me in flashes, the pain along with it. The rage in my mother's eyes. The sting of the glass.

An arm shifted around my waist and pulled me tighter against a muscled chest. Anson's familiar scent filled my nose. The form in front of me turned, seeming to follow us. Lucas' sandy brown hair and chiseled jaw came into focus, as his hand found mine under the covers.

My nose stung as my gaze swept over the rest of the room. Holden was asleep on some blankets on the floor, and Keene was curled up on a sofa. A burn lit in my throat as I took in yet another person at the foot of the bed.

Vaughn. He was rumpled, his black hair sticking up in every direction, and there was no way he could be comfortable. But he was here. He hadn't left.

"Ro?" Lucas whispered.

"Hi," I croaked, my eyes meeting those hazel ones.

His hand squeezed mine. "How do you feel?"

"Okay, I think." Better than I should've. My eyes and throat hurt from crying, but nothing else. There wasn't even an ache in my cheek.

I waited for shame or embarrassment to wash over me, at the guys having seen me fall apart like that, but it didn't come. For some reason, I felt safe letting them know exactly what a mess I was.

"You're not alone in this. We're going to figure it out together."

My head fell forward, resting on Lucas' bare chest. With his free hand, he stroked my hair.

Someone's phone alarm sounded, and Holden sat straight up, silencing it quickly. His gaze cut to me as I pushed up in bed. "Are you okay?"

"Yeah. I'm fine. Sorry about—"

"You never have to apologize. Not to us," Holden cut me off.

Something about that sent warmth flooding through my chest.

Vaughn stood up from the bed, surveying my face. "We should check your wounds."

I swallowed at the rage simmering in those ice-blue eyes. "Okay."

Anson sat up next to me. "Here. I'll take the bandage off. I didn't want to do it last night since you were finally resting."

He carefully peeled back the large covering. His hands froze as he lowered the gauze. "What the hell?"

I stiffened, sitting up straighter. "What is it? What's wrong?"

Holden and Vaughn were by Anson's side in a flash, Keene hovering behind them. Holden's eyes widened. "There's nothing there."

"What do you mean?" I scooted towards the end of the bed

and then hurried to a large mirror over a dresser. I studied my cheek in the reflection. The only thing that was there were two thin, red lines where the worst of the wounds had been. They looked like faint cat scratches.

My fingers lifted, slowly tracing the lines. There was no sign of a scar or anything else. I turned, facing the guys. "W-what's happening? What's wrong with me?"

Vaughn's gaze was hard. "Nothing's wrong with you."

"This isn't normal."

Holden took a step forward, a hint of concern flashing across his expression. "I think I know, but—"

"If you say that you can't tell me yet, I'm going to junk punch you."

Keene choked on a laugh. "She has a point, H. Ro deserves to know what's going on."

I straightened. "Thank you. Now someone freaking tell me."

"After school," Holden said. "We'll go to the compound and explain everything. But my father has to be there. We have no choice about that."

"He's right," Lucas said. "Mason has to be the one to tell you."

I searched the faces in front of me, trying to get any glimmer of a clue. Possibilities ran through my head, everything from me really being an alien, to having been bitten by a radioactive spider and not realizing it. I wanted to tell them to take me to Mason right now, but I didn't want to find out what would happen if the school called my mom and she found out I'd skipped.

"I want you to promise you'll take me right after school. No more lies and half-truths."

Holden inclined his head towards me. "You have my word."

I looked at the rest of the guys. "Do I need to get that in writing or is that enough?"

Anson chuckled. "Holden might be a lot of things, but he's always true to his word."

Holden sent Anson a glare. "Gee, thanks."

He shrugged. "You might be a suck-up golden boy, but you've got honor."

Holden took a step towards Anson, but I grabbed the back of his shirt and tugged him back. "Can we please, for the love of all that's holy, lower the testosterone for one day?"

Keene wrapped an arm around my shoulders. "I think that's gonna be impossible for the foreseeable future."

Great, just great.

CHAPTER THIRTY-TWO

"WHAT ARE YOU GUYS DOING?" I HISSED AS WE made our way down the hallway. They were encircling me like they were the Secret Service and I was the President. Anson was on one side, Keene on the other. Holden took up the front, and Lucas trailed behind. It wasn't like my mom was going to jump out of a classroom and throw another glass at my head.

Anson sent me a devilish grin and wrapped an arm around my shoulders. "What are you talking about?"

"There aren't assassins out to get me."

As soon as the words were out of my lips, my gaze locked with Sadie's livid one. Her eyes tracked over Anson's arm. *Great.*

She turned back to her huddle, whispering furtively.

"That's new," Keene muttered.

"What?" I asked.

He lifted his chin towards a head of brown hair in Sadie's bitch squad. Jasmine. "I didn't think she was friends with them."

Holden's jaw tightened. "She's not."

Apparently, I was the common enemy, bringing everyone together. Just grand.

The guys stuck so close all morning that I was almost tripping over them. If I left a class to go to the bathroom, one of them followed. When I'd gotten up to get a Diet Coke at lunch, Holden had escorted me. By the time I made it to English, I was ready to snap.

"I'll meet you here, right after class," Keene said.

"I don't need a babysitter," I snapped.

His eyes widened a fraction. "I know that."

I took a deep breath, letting it out slowly. "Then, please, stop hovering. I appreciate that you're worried, but I'm fine."

Keene gave me a sheepish smile. "Sticking a little too close?"

"Just a bit."

"Sorry. I'll tell the guys to back off a little."

I gave him a quick hug. "Thank you. I'll see you at the end of the day."

I hurried to find my seat, just as the teacher started speaking. Normally I liked English, but today I couldn't focus. Instead of listening to the teacher's lecture on *Emma*, I found my mind wandering to this afternoon. Nerves played a symphony in my stomach, a million possibilities running through my head.

The bell rang, making me blink a few times. It felt as if I'd just sat down. I hurried to gather my book and notebook, and slid them into my bag, not that I'd written anything down today. Maybe I could borrow notes from a classmate.

As I hurried out the door, the whispers started. I looked up to find the eyes of all the students in the hall pointed in my direction. Nausea swept through me as my gaze darted around.

"Do you think it's true? She killed her sister?" a girl whispered to her friend.

I jolted at her words, and I caught sight of a poster taped to a locker. I was moving towards it before I could stop myself. It was a black-and-white yearbook photo of me from my previous school, but scrawled across it in large red letters was *MURDERER*.

My hand shook as I reached it, tugging it down. But then I caught sight of another one. It was the same photo, but written on this one was *SISTER KILLER*.

Bile crept up my throat. Poster after poster lined the hallway. Each one with awful things written on it. I'd never get them all.

"Rowan!" Anson shouted.

I didn't want any more eyes on me. Eyes he would surely bring with him. I hurried down the hall, starting to run as I broke through the front doors of the school. The wind stung my face where tears had been falling without my knowing.

I heard shouts behind me, but I didn't stop, only pushing my muscles harder. I ran across the parking lot, dipping into a neighborhood next to the school, hoping I'd lose anyone who would follow.

My heart hammered against my chest as I ducked between houses. The sound of an engine had me dropping down behind a car. I watched as Anson's Range Rover passed. I waited for a minute and then rose. Listening, I counted to ten. When I didn't hear any other cars, I made my way back to the sidewalk.

I meandered through the neighborhood, slowly making my way towards home. But it didn't feel like home. It never had. It was this empty vessel that only reminded me what home used to feel like. A house that had been full of laughter and love. This one was only full of rage and grief.

There was a swift tug on my chest that I ignored. A reminder that the guys had begun to feel like home, and I had just run away from them.

Guilt pricked at my skin, but I ignored it and kept walking. Seeing them now would only make me break. And I didn't want to risk looking in their faces and seeing doubt there. Maybe I deserved to see that. Hadn't I been the one to kill Lacey? Sure, it had been an accident, a clueless deer springing out into the road, but she'd wouldn't have been there if it hadn't been for me. All for a stupid concert. I'd give back every show I'd been to, every song I'd heard, if it meant I could have her back.

The ache in my chest intensified as I reached home. I stared up at the gray house. I couldn't make myself go inside. I didn't want to face my mother, not like this, not after yesterday. Instead, I rounded the structure and headed through the backyard to the small path through the woods.

I needed that hit of peace—the roar of the water to drown out everything circling around in my brain. I dodged tree branches and roots until I reached the creek. I slid down onto the mossy embankment, letting the comforting scents of water and pine wash over me.

I tugged my legs to my chest and watched the water swirl, a kaleidoscope of colors. It was exactly how I pictured my grief, an angry mix of so many things. "I'm sorry, Lace," I whispered into the wind. "You'll never know how much."

A low growl sounded, and I froze. The fine hairs on the back of my arms stood on end as I slowly raised my eyes. There, on the opposite side of the creek, was a wolf.

It didn't look anything like the wolves in my dream. This one had his teeth bared and saliva dripping from them. His coloring was different too, a mix of browns.

Shit, shit, shit. Was I supposed to freeze or run? I'd never taken the time to research wolves like I'd told myself I would.

"Rowan!"

Vaughn's deep, familiar voice cut through the forest. He broke through the trees just as the wolf let another vicious growl free, his muscles bunching. "Get behind me," Vaughn barked.

I scrambled back. "W-what are you going to do? Do you have bear spray or something?"

Vaughn didn't answer or look my way; instead, he kept his gaze focused on the wolf. "You're trespassing on Ridgewood Pack lands. Leave now, and there won't be repercussions."

The brown wolf snarled, gnashing his teeth at Vaughn.

"I don't think he understands English, Vaughn."

The wolf paced back and forth on the other side of the creek.

"Go home, Rowan."

"I'm not leaving you here with a rabid wolf and nothing to defend yourself with."

"Rowan," he growled. "Go."

The wolf paused, its gaze going from Vaughn to me and back again. Then its muscles bunched and it sprung, leaping across the creek.

I screamed, the sound echoing off the trees around us. "Vaughn, run!"

He didn't run. He tossed his head to the side in an unnatural movement, and then there was no longer a man standing on the creek bank—there was a wolf. The same black wolf with the tuft of white on its chest from my dream.

The brown wolf lunged.

CHAPTER THIRTY-THREE

THE AIR IN MY LUNGS SEIZED AS THE BROWN WOLF SANK its teeth into Vaughn's flank. Vaughn. The ice-blue eyes were the same, but he wasn't a man anymore. He was a wolf.

My breaths came faster as the two wolves tumbled. Vaughn raked his claws across the other wolf's chest, making him howl. Instead of backing off, the wolf charged again, sending Vaughn flying.

As Vaughn tumbled into a roll, the wolf's head swiveled towards me. I swore there was a glint in his eyes as he did. I scrambled backwards until my back hit a tree. My hands frantically searched the ground for anything to defend myself with.

My palm landed on a stick, and I grabbed hold, swinging it out in front of me. "Back off."

The wolf let out a low growl, but it was cut off as Vaughn slammed into him, taking him to the ground. Something had snapped in my black wolf, snarls splitting the air as he tore into the brown wolf.

The brown wolf refused to submit, sinking its teeth into Vaughn's shoulder. I cried out as blood dripped from his wound. I pushed to my feet, tightening my hold on the stick and moving towards the fray. I wouldn't let Vaughn be seriously hurt, not because he was trying to defend me.

The fight was pure chaos and trying to find an opening to help was nearly impossible. But I braced myself, waiting. The brown wolf reared up on its hind legs. My opening. I swung the stick with everything I had in me, the wood cracking as it hit the wolf's spine.

He let out a howl, coming down hard and kicking back with his legs. They connected with my stomach, sending me crashing into a tree just as a voice yelled from the woods.

"Rowan!" Anson called.

"Help Vaughn!" I cried, my voice cracking on the words.

Holden and Anson came through the woods first, Lucas and Keene on their heels.

Holden took in the situation, and in a blink, he was gone, a golden wolf in his place. He snarled, leaping on the brown wolf's back as he tried to charge Vaughn again.

Anson's clothes ripped to shreds as he transformed from human into a wolf with a mix of black and gray fur. He let out a deafening howl.

The brown wolf's head snapped in his direction as Vaughn and Holden circled him. He let out a low growl and then leapt across the creek, taking off through the woods. Vaughn's muscles bunched as if he would follow, but Holden knocked into him, sending what looked like a silent command.

"Don't hit him," I yelled, clamoring to my feet. The world around me blurred a bit, and my hand went to the back of my head. Apparently, I'd hit the tree harder than I'd thought. "He's hurt."

Lucas and Keene reached my side. Keene steadied me, taking my arms. "Where are you hurt?"

"I'm fine, it's Vaughn."

Panic laced Keene's features as he turned to face his brother. Vaughn's breaths were labored, his black coat glimmering in the late afternoon light as his chest rose and fell in jagged movements. I started moving forward without thinking. I needed to get to him. To help.

Lucas caught hold of me. "You can't."

Vaughn let out a low growl, and Holden and Anson placed themselves between me and Vaughn.

"Stop it. He saved me and now he's hurting, we need to help." I tried to push forward, but Lucas held firm.

"Lucas is right," Keene said, so much pain in his voice. "You can't go to him now."

"Why not?"

Vaughn pawed the ground, snarling.

Keene didn't take his eyes off his brother. "He goes feral. He's barely holding on right now." Keene took a few steps forward, lowering himself so that he was eye to eye with Vaughn. There seemed to be a silent conversation between the two. Vaughn let out a low whine and then took off into the woods.

"But he's hurt. He needs medical attention."

Lucas pulled me into his arms. "He'll be fine. We heal fast in our wolf forms. But he needs to run off the feral edge. Otherwise, he'll never be able to shift back."

My head swam, not just with the hit I'd taken, but everything I'd seen in the past fifteen minutes. The wolves in front of me were just like the ones in my dream. It wasn't possible. Was I losing my mind?

"Ro?" Lucas asked gently as he tipped my head up.

"W-what's happening?"

He cupped my face with his hands. "I know it's a lot. This wasn't how we wanted to tell you."

"Y-you're a wolf? A werewolf?"

The corner of Lucas' mouth twitched. "We prefer the term *shifter*. We aren't beholden to a full moon like in werewolf lore. We can bring on the change any time we'd like."

I looked around, my gaze catching on the golden wolf and the salt-and-pepper one. They kept their distance but were on alert, gazes switching from me to the forest, and back again. "All of you are shifters?" I squeaked.

Lucas' gaze locked with mine. "We are. And you are too."

CHAPTER THIRTY-FOUR

I HADN'T SAID ANOTHER WORD. NOT WHEN LUCAS HAD asked if I was okay. Not when he and Keene had led me out of the woods to Anson's SUV. Not when Holden and Anson had reappeared fully dressed in different clothes, as if they hadn't gone furry thirty minutes before.

"You can drive, man," Anson said to Lucas as he climbed in the back seat. There wasn't the slightest bit of hesitation as he pulled me into his lap. He pressed his nose to the crook of my neck, inhaling deeply. "You scared the hell out of me. Please don't ever do that again."

I relaxed into his hold. As crazy and confusing as the past hour had been, it didn't change the fact that the only place I truly felt safe was when I was with one of these guys.

Holden got into the seat next to Anson and me, while Keene took shotgun. "Can we go to your place?" Holden asked.

Anson nodded. "Maxi is off this week because she's visiting her sister. No one will be there."

"Good." Holden's gaze swept over me. "Are you okay?"

I nodded against Anson's shoulder.

Holden reached out a hand, as if he was going to brush it over my cheek, and then stopped himself, dropping it to his side. Ever since that run-in with Jaz at the barbeque, things had been awkward between us. It was the last thing I wanted. It wasn't Holden's fault that he had a history with her. She'd been a friend to him when he'd needed it, and it wasn't fair of me to punish him for that.

I reached and took his hand, linking our fingers together. "Thank you for coming."

The deep blue of his eyes seemed to glow. "We'll always come for you, Rowan."

My throat burned at his words. "Don't make a promise you can't keep."

His hand spasmed in mine, but his gaze didn't waver. "There is a lot we'll have to go through. I won't lie to you and say it'll be easy. But we will always be there for you. You never have to doubt that."

Keene turned in his seat, his hand finding my knee. "He's right, Ro. You're stuck with us now."

Lucas chuckled as he caught my eye in the rearview mirror. "Hope you don't mind five tagalongs."

I had a million questions and didn't know where to start.

Anson nuzzled my neck, sending sparks across my skin. "We'll answer everything. Let's just get back to my place first."

"Okay." I let myself relax into his hold, and before I knew it, I was dropping off to sleep.

I curled into a muscled body. It certainly wasn't soft, but somehow, it still managed to be the coziest sleeping situation I'd ever experienced.

The chest below me rumbled with a chuckle. "You finally waking up?"

I blinked a few times, Anson's face coming into focus. "Hi."

He brushed the hair away from my face. "Hi." He pressed a kiss to my temple, and my heart ricocheted around my chest.

"She's waking up?" Holden asked as he strode into the living room.

"Yes," Anson grumbled. He bent, whispering in my ear. "Getting some one-on-one time with you is going to be a challenge."

My breath hitched.

"All right, Casanova," Keene said, dropping a hand to Anson's shoulder.

I straightened, sliding off Anson's lap to the couch, and positioned myself between him and Keene. "How's Vaughn?"

"I'm fine," Vaughn growled as he entered the room. His eyes narrowed on me. "You should've listened to me and run. You could've been hurt or killed."

"I wasn't going to leave you."

He prowled forward. "I can take care of myself. You clearly cannot."

Anson stood, stepping between us. "You need to back off, right now. The last thing Ro needs is someone yelling at her."

Vaughn's jaw hardened. "She needs to be yelled at if she has a prayer of surviving the year."

Holden let out an ear-splitting whistle. "Let's everyone dial it down a notch."

Lucas came in carrying a tray covered with snacks. "Let's eat. Hunger is only making this worse."

My stomach let out a loud rumble. Anson turned, his eyebrow quirking. "Was that you?"

My hands went to my stomach, pulling the blanket tighter around me. "I didn't have a lot at lunch."

Lucas wrapped a soft pretzel in a napkin and handed it to me. "Eat."

"I'll eat if you guys talk."

They all looked towards Holden.

I picked at the pretzel. "So you're in charge?"

He lowered himself to the coffee table so that he was directly facing me, as Lucas eased into a chair and Vaughn prowled. "My father is alpha, and I'm second in line."

"Alpha means leader, right?"

Holden nodded. "Coby is his beta or second-in-command. Sam is his third as head enforcer. But when I graduate, I'll take Coby's role and she'll take Sam's."

"And you've all always been…"

"Wolf shifters?"

I nodded.

"Yes. We were born this way. Wolf shifters can't be made. You were adopted, right?"

I stiffened, pushing myself back into the cushions on the couch. "I was, but I don't turn into a wolf, Holden."

Keene squeezed my knee. "The change isn't triggered unless you're around other wolves for at least a year. It's a self-protection thing."

"But you could be wrong. Why do you even think I could be one?"

"We can smell you," Holden explained.

"Smell me?" I squeaked.

His mouth twitched. "I smelled you that first day I saw you in your window. It was faint, but definitely wolf. Dad and I knew we had to find out if there was a new wolf family in town, but it was just you."

"What do I smell like?" I couldn't resist asking.

Holden's gaze locked with mine. "A field after a fresh, spring rain. And home."

Everything in me locked as I remembered walking into Anson's room and smelling home. "W-what does that mean?"

Anson's arm wrapped around me. "It means you're ours."

CHAPTER THIRTY-FIVE

"Yours? Like all of yours?" My heart hammered against my ribs. I swore I could feel myself being pulled in five different directions, soft tugs emanating from my chest.

Vaughn paused his pacing. "I'm not bonding with her."

The little bit of hope I'd been holding onto crumbled in my hands.

Keene pushed to his feet and stalked towards his brother, shoving his chest. "What the hell is wrong with you? I know you're scared, but that doesn't give you the right to be an asshole, not to Rowan."

"I'm not scared," Vaughn gritted out.

"Really? Because that's exactly what it looks like to me. I never thought my brother would be a coward."

Vaughn's nostrils flared, his gaze shooting to me. Then he turned on his heel and strode out of the room. A few seconds later, the front door slammed.

I sank deeper into the couch as Keene's shoulders slumped. Lucas stood, clapping his hand on Keene's shoulder and squeezing. "It's not your fault. He's not ready. But you know he'll only be able to hold out for so long."

Keene shook his head. "I've tried talking to him, but he refuses to listen."

I swallowed against the burn in my throat. "No one should force Vaughn to be with me if that's not what he wants." I struggled over the word *be*. What did that even mean in this situation?

Holden reached out, taking my hand in his. "That is what he wants. It's what we all want. It's fated."

"Fated?"

He gave me a gentle smile. "Did you feel something the first time you touched each of us?"

My eyes widened a fraction. "A spark."

"And something else?" Holden prodded.

I thought back to each time I'd felt the sensation. "With Vaughn, it almost hurt, like getting shocked. Lucas...I felt this warmth, I can't really explain it. When you and I touched, I couldn't move for a moment. With Keene, the rest of the world fell away. With Anson, I have no idea because my brain short-circuited."

Anson chuckled and nuzzled my neck. "Sorry about that."

"What does all that mean?" I asked Holden.

"It means you're our mate."

"Mate?" I curved my mouth around the word, testing out the sound of it.

He nodded. "It doesn't happen as often as it used to, but when a female wolf is especially powerful, she'll have multiple mates to ground her in her gift."

"I'm not powerful, Holden. I'm barely holding it together."

Lucas and Keene took a seat on my other side, Lucas' hand slipping into mine. "You're more powerful than you know. The wolves around you can sense it. I have a feeling it's why that wolf attacked today. He wanted to take you for his own."

172

"Take me?" I squeaked. "What does that even mean?"

Anson's grip on my shoulders tightened. "It means that we'll stick to your side for the foreseeable future."

My head was starting to spin. "Can we go back to the beginning? You think I'm a wolf shifter and your mate."

"We know it, Ro," Holden said as he squeezed my hand. "Look at me. Can you honestly tell me that you don't feel it too? That there's not a tug in your chest when you're not around one of us for a while?"

"H-how did you know that?"

"Because we feel it too," Holden explained.

"Only ten times worse," Keene muttered.

"Worse? Why didn't you tell me?" I hated the idea of any of them in pain. Even Vaughn, despite his asshole-ish tendencies.

Lucas traced a design on my palm. "You needed time. You've had so many changes to your life lately, and this is another huge one."

I sucked in a shuddering breath. He had a point. And if I hadn't seen it with my own eyes, I would've thought they were all crazy. "So my birth parents had to be wolf shifters?"

Anson toyed with a strand of my hair. "Only one needed to be. My birth father is a shifter, but my mom is fully human."

"Do you know who my parents are?" I asked, my gaze sweeping around the group.

Holden shook his head. "We don't. There are packs all over the world. Do you know where you were born?"

"No, just that it was a closed adoption." I'd never asked many questions about it because I hadn't wanted to hurt my parents. Now, I had a feeling they wouldn't give me the answers even if I did ask.

Holden squeezed my hand. "We'll talk to my dad about tracing your bloodline."

My stomach twisted. Was I ready for that?

Lucas must've sensed my panic because he gave my other hand a tug. "There's no rush with that. You have all the time in the world."

"Thanks," I whispered. "This is a lot."

"You know, Cass would be happy to talk to you if you have questions that you don't want to ask us." Holden's cheeks reddened as he spoke.

"How long has she known she had three mates?" I was curious how it worked for the wolves who had grown up in this life.

Keene shifted on the couch, turning to face me. "It wasn't long after she moved here. She started feeling a pull, and when she touched Ridge, Jack, and Cooper, they all knew."

"But how did she know it was three? Couldn't it have been more?"

The guys shifted nervously.

"What?"

Holden cleared his throat. "When the first bond forms, the female gets a mark somewhere on her body. It denotes the number of mates she is destined for. But it's rare to have more than three."

"Who else in your pack has five?"

"No one," Lucas answered.

Holden sat up, releasing my hand. "There's only been one bond of five before. I've never heard of a bond of six. Ever."

CHAPTER THIRTY-SIX

I WOUND THE TAILS OF MY BRACELETS TIGHTER AROUND MY finger. *I've never heard of a bond of six. Ever.* Holden's words echoed in my mind as we drove towards the compound.

Holden laid a hand over mine, stilling my movements. "Everything's going to be okay. I promise."

I threaded my fingers through his. "You don't know that."

"He does," Anson said from the driver's seat. "We'll make it so."

My lips twitched as I met Lucas' eyes in the rearview mirror. No one would ever accuse Anson of lacking confidence.

Holden cleared his throat. "I think we should keep the mate piece of things to ourselves for now."

A burn lit along my sternum. A secret. That was what Holden wanted me to be. Why? Because I wasn't raised in the pack? Because his father wanted him to be with Jasmine? I released my hold on Holden's fingers, sliding out of his grip.

"What the hell, H?" Keene barked from my other side.

Holden shifted in his seat, turning towards me and taking my hand again. "Ro, I want to scream from the rooftops that you're ours and we're yours, but as soon as word gets out that you have five mates, a target will be painted on your back. This is a lot all at once. I want to give you a chance to get used to being a shifter. Then we can tell the world."

Anson turned onto the dirt road that led to the compound. "He has a point."

Holden's gaze drifted out the window, a muscle in his jaw ticking. "I also don't want my dad meddling in this."

"Do you guys want this?" My voice was so soft, I could barely hear it myself, but four pairs of eyes shot to me as Anson pulled over to the side of the road.

Lucas turned in his seat. "I've never wanted anything more. You're a gift. More amazing than I ever thought possible."

"You understand me better than anyone ever has," Anson added. "And this is just the beginning."

Keene's hand wrapped around my thigh. "There's a connection with you I've never experienced before. But Anson's right. We're just getting started. It'll take time to figure out our dynamics. But don't doubt for a single second that we want you."

My eyes lifted to Holden's dark blue ones. "And what do you want?"

"You." His words were guttural, almost as if they were ripped from his throat. He framed my face with his hands, moving in so that our lips were so close, I could almost feel them. "I've never wanted anyone as much as I want you."

His lips brushed against mine, the barest of touches. Heat flooded me. Nerve endings I hadn't known existed sparked to life. On a growl, Holden deepened the kiss, his tongue tangling with mine. Heat grew low in my belly. I wanted more, to lose myself in him and never come up for air.

Someone coughed and I blinked a few times as Holden pulled back, his stare hooded. Keene hadn't released my leg, and I could feel the eyes of everyone on me. My face heated. I was expecting to see jealousy or anger when I looked at the other guys. Instead, I saw smug smiles.

I buried my face in my hands. "This is too weird."

Lucas chuckled. "Don't worry. You'll get used to it."

Keene swept his thumb back and forth across my thigh. "That was hot."

"Keene!" His name came out on a half-laugh, half-shriek.

He shrugged. "What? It's true."

"He has a point, Ro," Anson said as he pulled back onto the road. "Thought you were going to light up right there."

Holden wore a self-satisfied smile as he leaned back in his seat.

I glared at him. "You don't have to look so smug."

He leaned forward and pressed a kiss to my forehead. "Not smug, content. Never thought I'd feel this at peace after everything we've been through today."

His words had a flicker of dread trickling through me. "Do you know who that wolf was?"

Keene's hold on my leg tightened as the gate to the compound opened. "No. We've never seen him before."

"His scent wasn't familiar either," Holden added.

"So he could come back?" I asked.

Holden moved in closer. "Don't worry. You'll be safe. You'll have at least two of us with you at all times outside of school."

"But no more going off into the woods behind your house," Lucas said, turning in his seat to pin me with a stare.

"Trust me, I have no desire to do that anytime soon." But I would need alone time. I wanted it right now. Time to process the events of the past twenty-four hours and to try to wrap my head around an entirely new existence.

Lucas reached back and placed a hand on my knee. "Take a deep breath. You've got this."

I wished I could muster up a little of Lucas' certainty.

Anson pulled to a stop in front of the lodge. He didn't even get his SUV into park before Mason was charging down the front steps, Coby and Sam flanking him. "Is she all right?"

Holden climbed out of the SUV, and I reluctantly followed, even though the energy coming off Mason in waves had me wanting to hide in the trunk. "I told you she was fine, Dad."

Mason's eyes narrowed on his son. "Remember who is in charge here."

Holden's head lowered. "Sorry, sir."

Mason nodded and turned his focus to me. "You weren't hurt?"

I swallowed as Keene took my hand in his, and Anson and Lucas appeared at our backs. "Just a little bump on the head."

Mason's jaw worked back and forth. "This never should've happened."

"Did the patrols find anything?" Holden asked.

Mason nodded at Sam as if giving him permission to answer.

"We tracked the scent to a back road that leads to the highway. He must've had a vehicle waiting there for him because his trail disappeared." Sam's hard gaze gentled as he turned it to me. "I'm so sorry this happened, Rowan. We don't usually have strange wolves encroaching on our territory."

"Someone passing through must've scented her," Anson said, moving in closer to me.

Mason studied me carefully. "We can all sense power in you. Some will be intimidated by it. It'll ruffle others' fur, making them want to challenge you. And some might want that power for themselves."

I couldn't help the slight tremble that ran through me. Lucas stepped closer and took my other hand, squeezing it.

Coby looked down her nose at me. "That might be exaggerating things a bit, Mason. She hasn't even shifted yet. She could be latent, for all we know."

"Latent?" I asked.

Coby rolled her eyes. "A dud. A shifter who will never know what it is to run as a wolf."

Anson let out a low growl. "Don't speak to her that way."

Coby's stance changed, her shoulders rolling back. "Remember who's dominant here, pup."

Anson grinned, but it had a feral edge to it. "You sure about that, *beta?*"

Something flashed in Coby's eyes so quickly, I almost missed it. Doubt. She wasn't sure she could hold her own against Anson.

"Enough," Mason barked. "Both of you are acting like toddlers. Right now, we need unity and to welcome Rowan to her new family. She needs to be brought into the fold and protected until she can protect herself."

Family. My chest seized at the idea. I wanted it and yet was terrified. The reminder of my own family shattering had me reaching for the phone in my pocket. No text messages. If the school had called my parents, telling them I'd taken off for the day, my parents didn't care.

Lucas gripped my hand tighter and a soothing warmth spread through me. My eyes snapped to his. "What was that?"

He grinned sheepishly. "My gift. I'm an empath. I can ease intense emotions of those closest to me."

I looked at the people around me. "Do you all have gifts?"

Mason shook his head. "They aren't bestowed on every wolf. But our pack has been blessed with quite a few. Like the friends you seem to have made for yourself." There was an air of suspicion to Mason's tone, and I turned to study the guys around me.

"I can shield myself from offensive gifts, and sometimes Vaughn too," Keene said.

Holden's jaw worked back and forth. "I can control physical movements in others for brief periods, freezing them in place. But we can only use the gifts in human form, not when we're wolves."

Interesting. I turned to Anson. "And you?"

He shot me a cocky grin. "Strength."

"What about Vaughn?" I asked softly.

Everyone was quiet for a moment and then Keene spoke. "His gift is pain. He can inflict it with physical touch when his emotions are heightened."

I knew in an instant that Vaughn didn't view this as a gift. He viewed it as a curse. My heart ached for the broody bastard.

"We suspect you'll have a gift as well, and it will be quite interesting to see what it is," Mason said, bringing my attention back to him.

"You think I have a gift? I haven't even shifted."

"I actually think I might know what it is," Lucas cut in.

My head snapped in his direction. "You do?"

His hand brushed over my cheek where the slices had been just yesterday. "Healing."

CHAPTER THIRTY-SEVEN

COBY SUCKED IN AN AUDIBLE BREATH. "BULLSHIT."

Lucas' gaze hardened on her. "She healed herself overnight, and she took away one of my headaches."

Coby shook her head. "You're imagining things. There hasn't been a true healer in our pack in centuries."

Sam eyed me, not with doubt or derision, but curiosity. "Just relax, Coby. Whatever gifts Rowan has will make themselves known over time. But no matter what, she's one of ours now."

Mason sent Coby a charged look. "He's right and you would be good to remember that."

Coby gave a stiff nod. "I'm going to join the patrols."

Mason lifted his chin to release her and then looked to Sam. "Check in with the enforcers and report back in an hour."

Sam dipped his head. "Of course."

"Let's go inside and talk," Mason said.

We made our way up the stairs and into the lodge. It was remarkably quiet, but it was the middle of the afternoon. Mason led us to a large sectional in front of a fireplace. The guys positioned me in the middle—Holden and Keene on one side and Anson and Lucas on the other.

Mason's lips thinned as he studied us. "Tell me more about this healing."

Lucas told Mason about the cut on my face, leaving out that it was from a glass my mother had thrown. "And before that, we were studying and I had one of my headaches." He glanced at me. "I can get bad ones if I'm around too many emotions."

I thought about all the heightened emotions I'd exposed him to and winced. Lucas reached around Anson and squeezed my arm. "It's okay. I can handle it. But remember how you rubbed my head when we were at Anson's?"

"Yeah…"

"You took the pain away. Not just lessened it, but it was totally gone."

Mason studied me. "It would be wonderful if that were the case, but we can't know for certain."

"Yes, we can." Anson moved so fast, I barely had a chance to see what was happening. He pulled a pocketknife out and drew the blade across his palm. Blood pooled there.

"Anson!" My hands moved on instinct, covering his, wanting to take the pain away, hating that he was hurting.

His eyes met mine. "It's okay. I trust you and we need to know."

My heart hammered against my ribs. "I-I'm not—I don't have the first idea of what to do."

"Reach out," Lucas suggested. "Close your eyes and feel his pain. There is always a little bit of empathy in a healing gift. It'll be instinct for you to mend the wound."

I let my eyes close and tried to do what Lucas instructed. At first, all I could feel was my heart racing. I took a few slow, deep breaths and tried again. In the quiet, I could hear four hearts, almost as if they were beating alongside mine. I could feel a fifth one farther removed, and it hurt as I tried to pull it closer. Vaughn, I realized, tears stinging the back of my eyes.

I focused on the four that felt closer. There was a sort of energy that flowed between all of us. One strand pulsed, and as I zeroed in on it, I could feel the red heat of pain, a mirror of the slice in my own palm. My hands tingled as I thought about the flesh knitting back together, of pushing a golden light into Anson.

After a moment, hands landed on my shoulders. "That's enough, Ro."

Holden's voice brought me out of my trance, and I realized he was now standing behind me.

My gaze flashed to Anson. "Did it work?"

He pulled his hand slowly out from between mine, lifting it up for all of us to see. There was nothing there. No scar or evidence it had ever been injured.

"I can't believe it," Mason said quietly. "That kind of healing before she's even shifted?" He turned his focus to me, almost a little wariness there.

Holden dug his thumbs into my shoulders, massaging. "She's amazing."

Keene's hand wrapped around my thigh. "She really is."

"H-how?"

"I can't answer that," Mason said thoughtfully. "But it would help to know who your birth parents are."

"Are gifts like these passed down?"

Mason nodded. "They can be. Sometimes they're a melding of the two, manifesting in a different way. Other times, gifts can skip a generation or disappear altogether. Holden and I both have control as our gift."

"My adoption was sealed, so I don't know how we'd find out who my parents are."

"We have ways," Mason assured me.

My breaths started coming faster. I wasn't sure I was ready

for that. Being faced with people who were so willing to throw me away. I already had one family that had cast me aside, I didn't need the reminder of a second.

Holden's hands continued to dig into my shoulders, soothing away the worst of the tension there. "Dad, give her time. This is a lot."

Mason's eyes took on a hard glint. "Holden…"

His name was a warning, and Holden's hands dropped from my shoulders. "I know you're alpha. I respect that, but Rowan's my—" His words cut off for a moment. "She's my *friend*. I know what she's been through these past few months, and we just dropped a whole other life on her. You need to back off."

There was a slight vibration to the last of Holden's words. Mason's jaw tightened, but he inclined his head towards his son. "I'll give her some time, but not too long."

My shoulders slumped in relief just as my phone buzzed in my pocket. I pulled it out, scanning the screen.

Mom: *Where are you? You should've been home hours ago. Did you forget you're grounded?*

Crap.

Me: *I'm working on a group project for school.*

I nibbled on my thumbnail as I waited for a response. Anson slipped a hand under my hair, massaging my nape.

Mom: *You didn't get permission for that. Get home now.*

I blew out a breath, fluttering the hair around my face. "I need to get home."

The tension in the room ratcheted up as four sets of eyes bored into me.

"You are not going back there," Anson growled.

"I have no choice. I'm seventeen. I have to do what she says."

My stomach twisted as my mother's rage-filled face flashed in my mind. Maybe I could hole up in my room and barricade the door.

"What's all this about?" Mason asked, voice gruff.

Holden glanced at me, and I sent him a pleading look. "Rowan's mom isn't the greatest. She's been pretty cruel to her since Rowan's sister died."

Mason's expression softened. "I'm so sorry. Grief has a way of bringing people low at times. If you need a place to stay—"

"Thank you, but I really do have to go home. Asking to stay here will just make things worse."

Mason studied me carefully. "You'll tell me if things get too bad? There are things we can do."

Unless he had the ability to sober my mom up and snap her out of her hate-filled haze, or kidnap me, I wasn't sure he could help. But I appreciated the offer. "Thank you."

I looked to Anson. "Can you take me home?"

A muscle in his jaw ticked. "Sure."

I knew it was the last thing he wanted to do, but I'd have to face the firing squad eventually.

CHAPTER THIRTY-EIGHT

ANSON PULLED UP IN FRONT OF MY HOUSE. "ARE YOU sure you want to do this?"

I pulled my backpack onto my lap. "I don't have another choice."

"I hate this," Lucas grumbled from the back seat.

Keene and Holden had stayed back at the compound to help with patrols, and Mason had told me they would have wolves making the rounds in the woods behind my house all night. But it wasn't the wolf who'd attacked earlier today I was frightened of. It was the monster inside my own home.

"I'll go straight to my room, and I won't engage," I assured them.

Anson turned to face me. "Call me once you're in your room. I'll wait at the end of the block until we know you're okay."

"You don't have to—"

He leveled me with a stare. "It's either that, or I come inside with you."

Somehow, I didn't think that would go over too well with my mom.

Lucas leaned forward. "I'll be able to feel if anything happens."

My eyes flared. "Seriously?"

He sent me a sheepish smile. "You're my mate. From the first time we touched, I've been able to sense if you were especially upset or happy."

"That's how you knew to come after I got cut."

All humor fled his expression. "I didn't know what had happened, but I knew you were in pain. And you weren't answering your phone—"

I leaned towards Lucas, resting my forehead against his. "I'm sorry, Luc. I didn't mean to worry you."

"It's not your fault."

Reluctantly, I pulled away. "I should go. I don't want her to be more mad than she already is."

Anson gave me a quick hug, his heat seeping into my muscles. "Call us if anything at all feels off."

"Or if you just want someone to talk to," Lucas added.

"I will. Thanks." I slid out of the SUV before I had a chance to second-guess my decision. There was a swift tug on my chest as I walked up the path to my front door, and I rubbed my sternum, trying to alleviate the pang. It didn't help.

I pulled my keys out and unlocked the door. I shut it quietly behind me. But it wasn't quiet enough.

"Rowan," my mother snapped, her voice coming from the kitchen. "Get in here, right now."

I swallowed and moved towards the sound. She leaned against the counter, a bottle of some unnamed liquor and a half-empty glass at her side. "Who was that dropping you off?"

"My history group."

Her eyes narrowed on me. "Two boys?"

"There are three in the group actually."

She snorted. "I should've known you'd turn into a slut the first chance you got."

I sucked in a sharp breath at her words. "They're my study

group." And so much more. They were everything. But I couldn't tell my mother that.

"I'm sure you're doing so much *studying*. Were you taking turns fucking them when you skipped school today?"

My heart picked up its pace as I scrambled for any excuse. "I-I had a migraine. Holden offered to take me to his house so I could rest. His dad was there the whole time. Then we worked on our project when I was feeling better." I had to hope that Mason would cover for me if my mom called him.

She scoffed. "You always were a shit liar, Rowan. I've called your father to inform him how much trouble you've been lately. He thinks you're acting out due to grief. But I know the truth. You never gave a damn about Lacey." Her voice cracked on Lacey's name. "You don't even care that you killed her."

My mom's words cut worse than any glass ever could've. "I didn't," I whispered.

"What did you say?"

"I didn't kill her." My words were louder this time, my voice stronger.

Mom shoved away from the counter, her steps wobbling. "You might as well have stabbed her in the heart."

Tears burned my eyes, but I refused to let them fall.

"Your father's looking for treatment programs to send you to. Ones for delinquents just like you. It's not enough punishment, but it's something."

My ribs constricted around my lungs, and I couldn't get any air in.

"Get out of my sight!"

She shoved my shoulders, and I stumbled back a few steps. It was all I needed. I ran up the stairs, shutting my door and sliding the desk in front of it. It wouldn't stop her, but at least

I'd have a warning if she came in. My body trembled as I struggled to breathe.

My phone rang. It took a few tries for me to pull it out of my pocket. My fingers shook as I swiped my thumb across the screen to answer, but I couldn't get out a greeting.

Lucas' voice came across the line. "Ro, what happened? Where are you?"

"M-my room." I could barely hear my own hoarse words.

"I'm coming."

CHAPTER THIRTY-NINE

I DIDN'T HAVE IT IN ME TO GET ANYTHING ELSE OUT, BUT Lucas had already hung up. I simply stood there, mind swirling and lungs burning. I barely registered the window opening and then Lucas was in front of me, hands framing my face. "Let it out," he urged.

It came in a wave, and Lucas let out a grunt. The pain and fear. The sheer despair. Words came with it, all the awful things my mom had said.

He drew me into his arms. "We won't let them take you. I promise."

"You can't stop them. I'm not eighteen." I'd never wished for an earlier birthday more. One that would mean I could leave, go stay at Anson's, anywhere but here.

"Come on."

"I can't."

Lucas' hazel eyes flashed gold. "You can and you will. We'll bring you back tomorrow, but you're not spending the night here unprotected."

I didn't want to be alone here. I wanted to be in the only place I felt safe. With my guys.

"How? My mom is in the kitchen."

"We're going out the window. Remind me to thank the previous owners for putting in a lattice. Makes for easy climbing."

I let out a shuddering breath. "Okay."

Lucas tugged me towards the window. "I'll go first and then spot you on your way down."

I watched as he navigated the rungs of the lattice like it was a ladder, but when I climbed out, the distance to the ground looked impossibly higher.

"I won't let you fall," Lucas whispered, his words catching on the breeze.

I swallowed and began to climb down. I focused only on the next step, trying my best to ignore the forty-foot drop. Before I knew it, warm hands circled my waist, lifting me off the lattice.

Lucas took my hand, pulling me across the lawn and down the street. We jogged to Anson's SUV. I hurried to climb in, Lucas following.

"Drive," Lucas ordered.

He pulled away from the curb. "What the hell happened?"

Lucas pulled me into his lap, and I burrowed into his chest. "Ro's bitch of a mom is trying to send her away."

The low growl that filled the SUV had me jumping, but Lucas just pulled me tighter against him.

"It'll never happen," Anson gritted out.

"No, it won't," Lucas agreed.

I was too tired to argue, to point out how little power I had in all of this. I had no proof that my mother had turned into an abusive asshole, and I had no rights as a minor. I slumped against Lucas, soaking up his comfort and that buzz of energy that was only his.

Anson came to a stop in front of his house, not bothering to pull into the garage. I scooted off Lucas' lap and climbed out of the SUV. As soon as my feet hit the gravel, a bone-deep weariness swept through me.

Anson appeared in front of me. "Ro?"

"It's too much."

His expression softened. "I know, baby." Without another word, he swept me into his arms and headed inside.

I didn't protest as he carried me upstairs and deposited me on the counter in his bathroom.

"You want sweats or my boxers to sleep in?" he asked, as if we'd done this a million times before.

I thought about how hot I'd been when I'd woken up yesterday. "Boxers, please."

He disappeared for a moment and then reappeared with a T-shirt and black boxer briefs. "I'll be outside if you need me."

"Thanks," I croaked.

He shut the door and I slid off the counter. My movements were robotic as I stripped off my clothes and put on the boxers and tee. The whole time, my mother's words echoed in my head. They rattled around like a ball made of razor blades, ripping at anything they touched.

"Ro, you okay?" Lucas' voice came through the bathroom door.

Of course, he could feel that pain too. "I'll be out in a second."

I ran the water as cold as I could and splashed it over my face, trying to banish my mom's taunting tone. I patted my face dry and stared at my reflection. I couldn't help but see a stranger staring back. Too much had changed in the past few days. But not all of it for the worse. I had a chance for a beautiful life, with people who truly cared about me. I wouldn't let my parents take that from me.

I opened the bathroom door to find Lucas and Anson

waiting. Lucas' mouth curved the barest amount. "You found your mad."

"A little of it anyway. They don't get to take this from me. They don't get to take *you* from me."

"Damn straight," Anson said, as he pulled me into his arms and pressed his lips to my temple.

"But first, I need sleep."

He chuckled. "Sleep, we can do." He set me down. "You okay with Lucas and me sleeping with you?"

My cheeks heated, but I nodded. "I never feel safer than when I'm with one of you."

Lucas brushed his lips against my hair. "That's how it's supposed to be." He squeezed my waist. "Get in bed."

I climbed up onto the large bed that had to be a California King and crawled under the covers. My eyes flared as Anson pulled off his shirt, acres of golden skin on display. My breath hitched as his fingers went to his jeans, unbuttoning them.

The bed behind me dipped and Lucas' body curved around mine. I could feel the hard planes of muscle against my back, his skin soft and warm with a sprinkling of hair. His hand looped around my waist, pulling me closer to him. "I've got you," he whispered.

The sentiment was so simple, yet it made my nose sting and my eyes burn. "I know you do." I trusted it. Trusted all of them, in a way I never thought I'd be able to trust again.

Anson pulled back the covers and lay down next to us. He brushed the hair away from my face, his fingers trailing down to my neck. My nerve endings sparked to life as I felt the energy from both Anson and Lucas flowing through me.

Anson moved in closer, his mouth stopping just shy of mine, asking silent permission. I closed the distance. His lips were softer than I would've ever imagined. His tongue teased mine, starting an ache low in my belly.

Lucas traced circles on my stomach, and I could feel him harden against my backside. I arched back into him as Anson took my mouth.

Lucas let out a low groan. "God, Rowan. Everything about you feels perfect."

Anson pulled back, his eyes hooded. "Been wanting to do that since the first time I saw you."

Lucas' lips trailed down my neck, his hand moving lower. "What do you want, Ro?"

I let my eyes fall closed, sinking into the sensation of his fingers. "I want to feel."

"We can make you feel," Anson said, his voice husky.

He tugged at the hem of my shirt, lifting it over my head. The cool air met my bare breasts, my nipples tightening. Anson's thumb trailed over a peak, circling. "So fucking pretty."

My core tightened. "Lucas," I murmured.

His lips traced over the shell of my ear. "Need my fingers?"

"Yes."

His hand dipped into my boxers as Anson continued his exploration of my breasts. He rolled my nipple between his fingers, and I groaned.

Lucas' fingers slid down my center, two fingers slipping inside me. "Hell, you feel amazing."

Anson's eyes flared, the green glinting in the low light of the room. "Tell me."

Lucas' fingers began to move, in and out, in lazy strokes. "So tight and wet. I can't imagine what it'll feel like to be inside you."

I let out a whimper, arching further into him.

"More?" Lucas asked.

"More," I rushed out on a breath.

A third finger entered me as Lucas' thumb circled my clit.

I pulled in a sharp breath as Anson's lips latched onto my nipple. The zing of sensation went right to that bundle of nerves as Lucas stroked it. His fingers inside me curled, hitting a spot I hadn't been sure existed.

I reached deeper inside myself, pulling on that thread that Lucas and Anson had been weaving with their ministrations. Lucas pressed on my clit as Anson's teeth grazed my nipple. I fractured, everything inside me seeming to shatter. And I knew when I came back together, I'd never be the same.

CHAPTER FORTY

I WOKE AGAIN TO HEAT. MY FRONT PRESSED TO LUCAS' BACK, and Anson wrapped around me from behind. I only wanted to sink deeper into the sensation.

Anson's lips trailed over my shoulder. "Morning."

"Mmmmmmm," I grumbled.

He chuckled. "Not much of a morning person, huh?"

"I need at least two Diet Cokes first."

"Shhhhh," Lucas mumbled. "I was having a really good dream."

Anson's mouth worked its way up my neck. "Pretty sure that dream was a reality, man."

Lucas turned towards us, grinning. "I guess it was."

My phone sent out a series of beeps from the nightstand. My stomach sank. I'd hoped that Mom would still be sleeping off her hangover, but she must have realized I was gone. "Can you hand me that?"

Anson's lips thinned, but he nodded, reaching over and grabbing my phone. I took it, scanning the messages.

Dad: *Where are you?*

Dad: *You have thirty minutes to get home, or you won't like the consequences.*

Crap, crap, crap.

"I have to go." I scrambled towards the end of the bed, barely remembering that I was shirtless. I grabbed my clothes from Anson's bathroom. "Do you have a shirt I can borrow?"

I didn't want to put the maroon blouse on for a third day in a row, and I was keeping the boxer briefs. I hooked my bra and pulled on my jeans.

Anson appeared, handing me a Cloverdale lacrosse T-shirt. "Was it your mom?"

I shook my head. "My dad."

Lucas joined us, having pulled on a shirt and his jeans. "Is that good or bad?"

I nibbled on my bottom lip. "I honestly don't know. I think good. He'll keep Mom in line. I just don't know if he was serious about trying to send me away."

"Not happening," Anson gritted out.

Lucas pulled me into his hold and rested his chin on top of my head. "We'll stick close until you call us and let us know what's happening."

I fisted my hands in his shirt. "Thanks."

I could hear Anson in the background, moving around while he got ready, but I simply stayed where I was, letting Lucas' soothing energy flow through me.

I tipped my head back so that my chin rested on his sternum. "Does it drain you when you do that?"

He trailed a hand up and down my back. "Not little trickles of energy like that. But if someone is truly distraught or angry, it can take a toll."

I pressed a kiss to his pec. "I'm sorry."

"I'm not. It's worth it to be able to help those I care about."

I tugged him closer to me. "You've got a good heart."

He blushed a little.

Anson cleared his throat. "Let's go. The last thing we want is Ro's dad even more pissed."

He had a point. We hurried downstairs and out to the Rover. Anson made the drive in half the usual time, while Lucas called Holden to brief him on the situation.

Anson pulled to a stop in front of my house. "Want me to go with you? Help you explain?"

"I don't think that's a good idea." Reminding my father that I'd just spent the night with two boys when he was already pissed? Bad move.

Lucas leaned forward, brushing a kiss across my lips. "Try to remember to leave yourself open to me. I'll be able to read you better if you don't have your walls up."

"Okay."

Anson pressed a kiss to my forehead. "Call us as soon as you're done talking to them."

"I will." I opened my door and slid out before I could beg Anson to drive me away. My steps dragged as I walked up the front path, my feet feeling as if they weighed a ton.

The front door opened before my foot hit the first step. My father glared at me. "Do you honestly think I need this on top of everything else I'm dealing with? Your mother was worried sick about you all night."

She appeared behind him, out of his line of sight, but I could see the twitch of her lips. She wasn't worried. She was overjoyed there was a piece of evidence to support her tale.

"It wasn't my intention to make anyone worry, but Mom was drunk last night and I was worried she'd throw another glass at my head."

The color leeched from my mom's face. "Do you see what she's putting me through, Bruce? These hurtful lies."

There was a flicker of doubt in my dad's expression, but then it steeled again. "Get inside. Where were you last night?"

"I stayed with a friend." It wasn't a lie exactly. But I didn't think my dad was ready for the truth. That I had five mates and apparently would turn into a wolf sometime in the next year. I had to fight a giggle from erupting. A wolf. Five mates. I still hadn't wrapped my head around that one. Yet, it felt right.

"She stayed with *boys*," my mother gritted out. "Rowan's sleeping around. She'll probably get pregnant, and then we'll have to raise another baby that isn't ours."

Her words didn't cut nearly as deep as they normally did. Maybe because I had a support system now, a team. My guys would have my back no matter what, and her cruelty didn't pack nearly the same punch when I was holding on to that knowledge.

"Cynthia," my dad clipped. "That's uncalled for."

Mom pulled her robe tighter. "You haven't been here. You don't know what all she's put me through."

My dad pinched the bridge of his nose. "Did you stay with boys last night, Rowan? Without informing your mother or me?"

I met his gaze dead-on. "You don't answer my calls or texts, so how do you suggest I inform you?"

"Don't talk back to me. I am the parent here."

"Then act like it! Or leave me the hell alone." I was sick of this messed up excuse for a family. "You're never here. Mom is falling apart and turning into someone I don't even recognize. You didn't even bother to call me on Lacey's birthday. You don't get to play the father one second and then disappear for weeks on end."

Redness crept up my dad's throat. "You're right. You clearly need some stricter discipline. Give me your phone."

"What?"

He held out his hand. "I said, give me your phone."

"I need it." It was my lifeline. If I didn't call Lucas and Anson, they would panic.

"You should've thought of that before you snuck out. Things are going to change around here. For now, you're grounded. Go to your room. It's that or we send you to that program your mother found in Montana."

My throat tightened, but I pulled my phone out of my pocket and dropped it in my dad's hand. My eyes burned. "Maybe you should consider that I'm telling the truth."

His eyes flashed. "Your mother would never harm you in any way. She loves you."

Mom pulled her robe tighter, disgust filling her eyes.

I didn't look away from my dad. "She used to."

CHAPTER FORTY-ONE

I TREMBLED AS I LOOKED OUT MY WINDOW FOR THE hundredth time. Dad had apparently taken down the lattice before I'd even made it home. I studied the tree in our front yard, but it was too far for me to make the jump. I shuddered, my chest aching. Something was wrong with me. The flu maybe? The world around me swam, and I stumbled back to my bed, curling into a ball.

Everything hurt. I pulled the blanket up with one hand as my stomach pitched and the pain in my chest intensified. I focused on trying to lower the walls Lucas had talked about. I sent him silent message after silent message, though I wasn't sure what he could do. Dad had informed me the alarm would be on all night, and he'd changed the code.

My stomach cramped and I cried out. There was a knock on my door. I couldn't manage to get words out as pain rocked through me.

Dad poked his head in. "Are you sulking?"

"Sick," I gritted out.

He moved into the room, studying my curled form. He brushed a hand over my forehead and even that gentle touch hurt. "You are a little warm and clammy."

"I need to call Lucas." I knew Lucas could help. At the very least, he might be able to sense what was wrong with me.

The little sympathy on my father's face vanished. "If you're sick, the last thing you need to be doing is infecting your boyfriend."

"Please, Dad."

"No, and that's final. I'll go get you some flu medicine and orange juice."

My body shook uncontrollably, fever or something else, I wasn't sure. There was no longer an ache in my chest—it felt as if the contents of my rib cage were being shredded. I whimpered into my pillow as my vision tunneled.

The doorbell rang downstairs, but I could barely hear it, everything seeming to be muted for a moment. Muffled voices became clearer.

"Hello, Mr. Caldwell. I'm Holden. We met a few weeks ago? I was hoping I could speak to Rowan for just a moment. It's about a school project. It's important."

"Unfortunately, Rowan is sick. She's also grounded. So, any visits will be impossible."

"Sick?" Holden's voice cracked on the word.

"Yes, some sort of flu," my father answered.

"I just need to see her for a minute. I have a great immune system, so I'm not worried."

"And I said, I'm afraid that's impossible. You'll have to leave."

Another whimper slipped out of my lips. He was so close. Something told me I just needed to get to Holden. If I could get to him, everything would be okay.

Footsteps sounded on the stairs, and my mother appeared. "Where is your second phone? I know you called that boy."

"I didn't," I croaked.

"Bullshit." She started pulling open drawers and throwing things on the floor.

Another spasm rocked my body, emanating from my chest. Whatever this was felt like it might kill me. I tried to focus on an image of Lucas, on what his comforting energy felt like. I just had to reach him. I swore I could feel tendrils of that energy just out of my grasp.

"What are you doing?" my dad asked as he entered my room, a glass of juice in hand.

"She's getting in touch with those boys somehow. She must have a hidden phone here somewhere." Mom pulled all of my clothes out of my closet and threw them on the floor.

I curled tighter into a ball. I just needed everyone to be quiet. Black spots danced at the sides of my vision. I wanted to sink into that darkness and let it swallow me whole.

"Rowan?" Dad's voice sounded farther away. His hand brushed my forehead again, and I pulled away. It felt like sandpaper against my skin. "I think we might need to take her to the hospital. She's burning up."

My mom scoffed. "She's faking. Trying to get you to feel bad for her."

"What's gotten into you, Cynthia?"

Mom began pulling books off my shelves and throwing them on the growing pile. "I see her for what she is."

The doorbell rang again.

"Get the door," my father commanded.

"I'm busy. You can get it," Mom retorted.

There was a knocking as my dad gaped at my mom.

"Hello?" A deep voice called from downstairs. Mason. Something in me was comforted at the knowledge of his presence, but it wasn't enough. My insides were being ripped apart.

My mom stiffened. "Did someone just let themselves in?" She shot me a hateful look. "These are the kinds of people you invite into our lives?"

Dad strode through my door. "Who is it?"

"I apologize for the intrusion," Mason said, his voice getting closer. "But my son is concerned about Rowan. I thought I'd stop by and make sure everything was okay."

"Get out!" my mother roared. "This isn't your house, and Rowan is none of your concern."

"Cynthia!" my father shouted, sounding stunned and appalled.

Another jolt of pain rolled through me, and I cried out. Couldn't hold it in no matter how hard I tried.

Footsteps sounded on the stairs, only it couldn't have just been one person. It had to be more.

"What are you doing in here?" Mom shrieked. "Bruce, call the police."

Cool hands framed my face, ones that didn't feel like sandpaper. "Rowan." My name was ripped from Holden's throat.

"She needs skin-to-skin contact," Lucas said, his hands dipping beneath my T-shirt and pressing into my back.

I let out a whimper as Holden pressed his forehead to mine. "What the hell did you do to her?" he barked.

"W-we didn't do anything." A hint of fear trickled into my father's voice. "She's sick, like I told you. Now, I'd like to know what you're doing here."

I could just make out Mason as he stepped forward. "Your wife has been abusing Rowan. It's time you protect your daughter."

A high-pitched shriek sounded, and my mom flew at Mason.

CHAPTER FORTY-TWO

OUT OF THE CORNER OF MY EYE, I SAW MY DAD CATCH my mom around the waist, just before her nails made contact with Mason's face. Mason didn't even blink.

"Cynthia!" Dad pulled her away from Mason as she struggled to get free. "What the hell is wrong with you?"

"Get them all out!" Her gaze swiveled towards me, and I could feel the hate pouring off of her in waves. "She's a murderer! She killed my baby!"

Dad stiffened as my mom broke down in tears, going limp and collapsing onto the floor.

Holden nuzzled the side of my face. "You're okay. We've got you."

It no longer felt as if the contents of my chest were being shredded, but pain still racked my body. "Hurts," I mumbled.

"I know. I'm so sorry."

Lucas rubbed circles on my back. "Everything will ease with a little time." His voice was strained, and I knew he was trying to take as much of the pain as he could.

"Don't, Luc," I whispered. "I don't want you to hurt."

He moved in even closer. "I'd do anything for you."

My eyes burned as a few tears slipped free.

Mason cleared his throat. "Your wife needs serious medical help."

Dad's eyes cut to Mason, hardening. "You don't know my wife." He bent to help my mom to her feet, as if picking her up would make everything fine and dandy.

"No, but I know your daughter, and I know that Cynthia has been putting her through hell. I should've stepped in before now, but I honestly didn't know it had turned physical. I thought Rowan could handle it until she graduated. That obviously isn't the case."

Dad's chest puffed up. "My wife is grieving. She might have said things she doesn't mean, but she'd never hurt Rowan."

Lucas jumped to his feet. "She threw a glass at Rowan's head. She could've killed her."

As soon as Lucas' hands left my skin, the pain intensified, and I couldn't help the whimper that escaped. Lucas muttered a curse and hurried back to me, giving me that skin-to-skin contact again. "Sorry, Ro. I'm here."

"Your wife needs medical intervention, inpatient care. I can recommend some places in Seattle, and Rowan is welcome to stay with us while Cynthia gets the help she needs."

"My wife doesn't need a hospital. She needs time. That's all."

Mom wobbled on her feet but took two steps towards me. "It should've been you. I'd give anything to have you be the one in the ground. Not my beautiful Lacey."

Mason's eyes flashed. "That isn't grief. That's sickness."

A flicker of guilt passed over my father's face. "Cynthia, go to our room. You need to lie down."

She whirled on him, almost losing her balance. "You! You don't even care. Lacey's dead, and you don't give a damn. You make me stay in this house with that girl. You never come home.

You're probably fucking your secretary. I don't even care. I just want Lacey back."

A muscle in my dad's jaw flickered, and he took hold of her arm. "You need to come with me."

She ripped her arm out of his hold. "Don't touch me. You're the one who wanted another kid. You couldn't be happy with just Lacey. You wanted more. Well, your more killed our baby."

She ran from the room, a door slamming downstairs moments later. The rest of us were silent. Lucas and Holden were still stroking me, trying to soothe the worst of my pain.

Dad lifted his chin. "I apologize—"

"Don't apologize. Get your wife the help she needs and give Rowan time to heal. Let her stay with us while Cynthia gets treatment."

My dad turned towards me, his gaze catching where Lucas and Holden's hands were on me. Nothing about the touches was inappropriate, but I knew they had to look odd to him. "Do you want to go stay with Mason and Holden for a little while? Just until I get Mom settled?"

"Yes," I croaked. He spoke as if Mom could get a shot and be back to normal by the end of the week. It wouldn't happen. If she could be helped, it would take a long time.

"Okay." He turned back to Mason. "Thank you—I don't know—"

"You don't have to say anything. I know what it's like to lose someone you love. Life can turn upside down for a while. Now it's your job to right it."

Dad nodded jerkily. "I will. I'll make sure Rowan has a credit card for expenses and to contribute to groceries or anything else."

Mason waved him off. "Don't worry about that."

"No, I want to cover her expenses."

"All right," Mason agreed. "Why don't you go sit with Cynthia for a while. The boys can help Rowan to the car. I'll write down those treatment centers for you and send someone over to pick up Rowan's belongings."

"Thank you." Dad moved towards me, and I could feel Holden and Lucas tense. "I'm sorry, Rowan. I didn't know how bad it was."

Of course he didn't. He'd been too worried about himself and numbing his own grief.

"Just get her help, Dad."

"I will. And I'll text or call to keep you updated."

"Okay." I turned into Holden's neck. I didn't want to hear my dad's promises. Ones that would likely never be fulfilled. I only wanted out of here. To feel safe and held.

"Call if you need anything," Dad said.

I didn't reply and eventually heard his footsteps retreat.

"Let's move before he changes his mind," Mason said briskly.

Holden slid his arms under me. "I'm going to pick you up, okay?"

I nodded.

Holden lifted me, and as Lucas' hands slipped away, the pain worsened again. I bit my lip to keep from crying out.

Holden pressed his lips to my forehead as he carried me out of the room and down the stairs. "Just stick with me, Ro."

Lucas ran ahead, opening the front door.

Three massive guys paced the walk. As soon as they caught sight of us, they rushed forward.

"What the hell happened?" Anson barked, his hand going to my cheek.

I almost sighed as his skin met mine, and I could see a similar relief in his expression. All the guys looked a little rough, actually. Pale, with dark circles rimming their eyes.

"We need to get her to the SUV," Holden said.

Vaughn filled my vision. He reached out as if he might touch me, but stopped himself. "Are you okay?" The words were jagged, as if torn from his throat.

"I'll be fine." I lifted a hand, pressing it to his neck.

"Don't," Vaughn growled.

"You won't hurt me." I knew now that so much of what held Vaughn back was out of fear, but the second I had that contact with him, more of my pain eased.

More of the tension slid away, and there was a look of wonder on Vaughn's face.

"Let's get her to the car. She needs to rest," Keene said.

"Keene," I said softly.

He moved in, ducking his head and brushing his lips across mine. "I'm so sorry, Ro."

"Not your fault."

His jaw clenched. "Maybe not, but we should've been here to stop it."

CHAPTER FORTY-THREE

I INHALED DEEPLY AS I SETTLED AGAINST THE PILLOWS ON Holden's bed. The room had a hint of pine to it, just like Holden himself. And like Anson's room, it smelled like home. Not a home that was four walls, but a home that was found in your soul. Peace and safety, and I was starting to believe…love.

Vaughn tugged at one of the huge socks I'd put on. Borrowed along with a pair of Holden's sweats and a T-shirt. His thumbs dug into the arch of my foot, and I let out a little moan. His lips twitched.

Anson moved in closer on one side of me, twining our fingers together. "You making sounds like that is torture."

"Sorry?" I said it like it was a question, and Keene laughed as he traced invisible designs on my forearm.

"Don't listen to Anson. He's clearly a wimp."

"No, I've just been a walking hard-on since I first saw her, and that starts to get painful."

Lucas choked on a laugh. "I don't need those kinds of details, man." He lifted the leg of my sweats and began massaging my calf. "How are you feeling now?"

"So much better." It wasn't a lie, the worst of the pain was gone. Now, it felt more like I'd had an epic case of the flu. My muscles ached and my throat was raw but it was manageable.

Holden appeared in the doorway, carrying a tray. "This should help even more."

Keene stood, clearing a spot on the nightstand for the tray.

"We've got chicken soup, fresh bread, and some orange juice. If this settles okay, I'll get you something heartier."

The scent of the soup and fresh bread filled my nose, and my stomach rumbled. "That smells amazing."

Holden grabbed a kitchen towel from the tray and spread it over my lap. "Here." He carefully handed me the bowl and a spoon. "Just let me know if you want bread or juice."

"I could eat this downstairs, you know. I'm not dying."

The room went silent, and my gaze swept over the guys.

"I'm not, right?" A hint of panic bled into my voice.

Lucas' hold on my calf tightened. "You're not."

Vaughn released my foot, sitting up. "But you could've. That's what he's not telling you."

"What?" My gaze instinctively jumped to Holden. He was the one who always seemed to have the most information, maybe because he was the alpha's son.

Holden glared at Vaughn. "You don't need to fill her head with that shit."

"She deserves to know the truth. The bonding process has started, whether we want it to or not."

"What is he talking about, Holden?"

Holden scrubbed a hand over his jaw. "It doesn't usually happen this way. When there's a true mate bond, you can feel sick if you're apart for too long, but this was different. We could feel your life force draining."

The spoon I held rattled against the bowl, and I set it down on my lap. "Why was this different?"

"We don't know," Holden answered. "But my dad is doing

some research to try to find out. It might be because you're so strong."

"I don't feel very strong right now."

Anson brushed his lips across my temple. "You are." He picked up my spoon and filled it with soup. "And to stay that way, you need to eat." He blew on the broth and held it up to my lips.

I didn't think I could force it down, not when there were so many unknowns swirling around us. But when the delicious soup touched my tongue, my stomach growled again. I took the spoon from Anson and kept eating. After downing the juice and the bread, I felt like a new person.

Holden smiled as he took the bowl from my lap. "Feel better?"

I nodded. "Thank you for all of that. It was amazing."

"Anytime."

Holden adjusted himself on the bed so he was even closer, his heat seeping into me. I had all my guys clustered around me. Vaughn at the foot of the bed, no longer touching me, but close. Keene had one of my legs in his lap. Lucas continued to massage my other calf. Anson linked my fingers with his.

I'd never felt more at peace than I did in this moment. I had no idea what was to come, but I knew I wasn't alone.

"Do you want to sleep?" Lucas asked.

I shook my head. "Not yet." I wanted to soak up this feeling, to store it in my muscle and sinew, so I'd never forget.

"Movie?" Keene suggested.

"A movie sounds perfect."

Anson straightened so that he could look down at me. "Please don't make me watch some sappy sob-fest."

Vaughn's lips twitched. "Scared of shedding a few tears?"

"Nah, man. I just don't want to become a human tissue."

I shoved at his chest. "I'm not going to snot on you."

"You say that now…"

"I think we need funny," I cut Anson off before he could give me any more of a hard time.

"Funny sounds perfect," Holden said, standing from the bed. He moved to the entertainment console and grabbed a remote.

As we bickered back and forth about what movie to watch, I couldn't help but be struck by how normal this felt. Fear gripped my heart. This normal was so beautiful, one that I could so easily sink into. But what would I be left with if it all fell apart?

CHAPTER FORTY-FOUR

I TRIED TO ROLL OVER BUT COULDN'T MOVE. FOR A MOMENT, panic flickered through and then that scent of home hit my nose. I relaxed again, pushing back into Keene's hold. He nuzzled my neck, inhaling deeply. My arm was draped over Lucas in front of me, my hand beneath his T-shirt.

Anson groaned from somewhere behind me. "How did I get the short end of the stick?"

"You got to sleep next to Ro last night," Keene answered.

Had that really been just last night? My blood heated at the reminder of coming alive under Anson and Lucas' touches.

Lucas rolled over and pressed a quick kiss to my lips. "Morning."

I put a hand in front of my mouth. "Morning."

He grinned wider. "I don't care about your morning breath."

"Well, I do."

Keene pulled me tighter against him. "You two can go. Rowan and I will go back to sleep."

I glanced around the room. Holden and Vaughn were nowhere to be seen. The clock on the nightstand read 10:30, and I sat up. "I can't believe we slept that late."

Lucas scooted off the bed and picked up a duffle by the door

"Cass went with Ridge and got your stuff yesterday. The essentials are in here."

I swung my legs over the side of the bed and stood. "Thanks. I'm just going to…" I pointed to the bathroom.

Lucas shooed me off. I shuffled into the bathroom, closing and locking the door. I made quick work of taking a shower and getting ready. My muscles were a bit stiff, but none of the pain remained.

Searching through my bag, I picked out jeans and a simple T-shirt, hoping it would be appropriate for whatever the day brought. I pulled my phone out of my bag and checked my messages. There was one from my dad from last night.

Dad: *I will be dropping your mom at an inpatient treatment program for acute grief in the morning. I will stay at the apartment in the city so I can be close if she needs me.*

If she needed him. What if I needed him? I was supposed to be his daughter, but I guessed I wasn't even that anymore. My fingers hovered over the touch screen.

Me: *I hope she's okay.*

It was all the truth I could give him. I didn't want my mom to drown in grief and hatred for the rest of her days, but I couldn't deny all the hurt they'd both caused, either. I shoved my phone back in my bag and opened the door.

The bedroom was empty, and I paused for a moment, listening. Soft strains of voices sounded from out in the hall. I set my duffle down at the foot of Holden's bed and headed out.

I moved down the hall and towards the stairs, the voices getting louder. As I reached the landing, I heard a hand slap some surface. "I don't give a damn. You should've told me the moment you realized she was your mate."

Mason's voice ricocheted through the space.

"I'm sorry. I just wanted to give us time to figure this out and make sure we were right. I've never heard of someone having five mates before," Holden said.

Mason let out a growl that made the fine hairs on my arms stand on end. "I could've helped you navigate the process if I'd known. Then we wouldn't have had to deal with the clusterfuck that was yesterday. Do you know what would've happened if Rowan had died? Likely, all of you would have too."

"What?" The single word was out before I could stop it as I descended the final stairs.

Six sets of eyes swiveled to me.

"She moves like a freaking ninja," Keene muttered.

I scowled at him. "You wouldn't have to worry about that if you weren't talking about me behind my back." My gaze turned to Mason. "What do you mean, they could've died?"

Mason ran a hand through his hair, tugging on the ends. "Your ties are stronger than any I've ever seen, even without the bond being cemented. You're already impacting each other strongly."

"You mean that they got sick when I did?"

"That and their gifts are stronger when they have pro-longed contact with you. Typically, that only happens after you're bonded."

I looked around the room, stopping briefly on each of them. I halted altogether when I came to Vaughn. There was a war going on within him. Anger and fear seeming to dominate.

"I can't do this. I don't want to hurt you," he said quietly.

"You haven't. Not once."

"What about when I first touched you? I saw the pain in your face."

"That was nothing." I took a step towards him, but Vaughn held up a hand, backing away.

"You don't know. I've killed people before. I won't do that to you." He turned on his heel and strode out the back doors of the lodge.

The tugging sensation in my chest was back, but it was so much more. My heart broke for Vaughn—the weight he carried and the self-hatred I could see flowing through him, clear as day.

Keene moved in close to me. "Give him time, Ro. He needs to wrap his head around this. He'll get there."

I pushed into Keene's side as he wrapped an arm around me. "I know. I don't want to push, but I don't want him to hurt like this. He thinks he's bad when he's anything but."

A tremor ran through Keene. "I hope you can make him see that. I've been trying for the past nine years."

I nuzzled Keene's neck, the way the guys so often did to me. The sensation was incredibly comforting, and I wanted to give Keene some of that reassurance. He pressed his lips to the top of my head in thanks.

I looked at the rest of my guys and Mason. "You keep talking about cementing the bond. How does that happen?"

Holden shuffled his feet. "It depends. Sometimes it's emotional, sometimes physical. It's different for every mate in the bond."

My cheeks heated as Holden mentioned something physical triggering the bond. Just what I wanted, to talk about sex in front of one of my boyfriend's fathers. I willed my voice to hold steady. "And there's a mark, right? That's how we'll know it's started?"

"The mark will appear when you bond to your first mate," Anson explained. He sent me a cocky grin. "You can bond with me any time you want."

Lucas smacked him upside the head. "Shut it."

"Hey, I'm just saying I'm willing."

Holden moved in closer, running a hand along my jaw to the back of my neck. "It'll happen when the time is right. Usually after you've had your first shift, which won't be for another nine months, at least." He brushed his lips against mine. "But none of that changes that you're ours and we're yours."

"You have got to be fucking kidding me."

Wonderful, Jasmine was here.

CHAPTER FORTY-FIVE

JASMINE LET OUT A GROWL FROM DEEP IN HER THROAT. *Shit.* Was she about to shift? All of a sudden, I was hit with the fact that I knew next to nothing about this world. Could Jasmine attack just for the hell of it? I didn't exactly have the means to defend myself.

Holden and Keene moved in even closer, positioning their bodies so that they were between me and Jasmine. I felt heat at my back and knew Lucas and Anson were there.

Jasmine sneered. "Do you really expect me to believe that she has four mates?"

"Five," Anson stated matter-of-factly.

Something shifted in Jasmine's gaze, almost an uneasiness. "Bullshit."

Coby appeared behind her daughter, placing a hand on her shoulder. "Take a breath. We'll sort this out."

Holden raised his chin, eyes glinting. "There's nothing to figure out. Rowan is our bond-mate, and she will be respected as such."

There was a trickle of energy I sometimes felt from Mason in Holden's words. Coby seemed to struggle against some invisible force before her head dipped. Her gaze cut to Mason. "You can't honestly believe this is true."

Mason stood tall, his focus assessing. "I've seen it with my own eyes."

"That kind of thing can be mistaken at this age. Their hormones are raging."

Keene let out a low growl. "Don't insult us."

Coby snarled in return. "Shut your mouth, pup."

Holden stepped away from me and prowled towards Coby. "I've had enough of your disrespect. You're power-hungry, always have been. Everything about you is desperate and reaching."

Coby gritted her teeth. "I'm still beta of this pack. You will show me some respect."

"Not for long, you aren't. And you forget that I'm stronger than you." His eyes began to glow, and Coby was frozen in place, her eyes wide. Holden moved in so that he was only a breath away from her. "I could gut you where you stand. I don't because I have more honor than you."

The glow in his eyes waned, and Coby stumbled back. She turned to Mason. "You would let him treat me this way? Your second-in-command?"

"Holden is the future alpha of this pack. I would never stop him from putting someone in line for showing his bond disrespect."

"She isn't his mate!" Jasmine cried, moving towards Holden and grasping his arm. "It's you and me. That's how it was always supposed to be."

I couldn't help the growl in the back of my throat at Jasmine's hand on Holden.

He pulled his arm from her grasp. "This is destined by fate. You and I were never meant to be. We aren't even friends anymore. You stopped truly listening to me a long time ago, too caught up in your mom's power-hungry plans for the future. You don't care about me. You only care about being Luna of this pack."

She reared back, as if Holden had slapped her. "That's not true."

"Really think, Jaz. Do you even know me anymore?"

"Of course I do. I know you better than anyone."

His eyes narrowed on her. "Then why have you been making my life ten times harder than it needs to be right now? Why have you been hurting the person I care about most? I asked you to make Rowan feel welcome. Instead, I smelled your scent all over those ugly posters at the school. Teaming up with Sadie and her crew should be beneath you."

Jasmine flushed, looking away.

The posters felt like a lifetime ago, and so unimportant, given all I'd found out recently. But the knowledge that Jasmine wanted to cause me as much pain as possible, I wouldn't forget. She'd known that my life was about to be rocked by finding out I was a shifter, she'd known that I was already hurting from losing my sister, and she had only wanted to intensify my pain.

I pushed forward, stalking towards her. "I haven't done anything to you."

Her eyes flashed. "You stole him. Came in with that whole 'wounded bird' act, and of course, Holden jumped. He's a natural protector."

"He was never yours to begin with." Even with as little as I knew about this new world, I knew that was true. Holden and Jaz had never even been together. They were friends. But it wasn't a true friendship if she was acting this way when he found the person he was meant for.

Her jaw clenched, and she faced Holden. "Are you se-riously going to throw away everything we've had for *her?*" Her bravado slipped a little, tears filling her eyes. "You were the only one who was there for me when my dad bailed. You taught me how to fight and defend myself so I wouldn't be the weak link in the pack. So that I could be worthy of a powerful mate. Don't do this, H."

I saw a little of Holden's resolve slip, and it crushed some-thing deep inside me. "I'm not trying to hurt you, Jaz. But I'm meant for Rowan."

He hadn't said he loved me or wanted to be with me, but that he was meant for me. Was that all I was to Holden? A duty?

Tears slid down Jasmine's cheeks. "I can't stand around and watch it."

She turned and tore out of the lodge.

Coby glared at me. "I hope you're happy. It wasn't enough that you destroyed your own family? Now you have to come in and destroy ours?"

I felt as if I'd been slapped.

Holden started after Coby as she followed her daughter, but Mason grabbed his shoulder. "Let her go, son."

Holden turned angry eyes on his father. "She can't be al-lowed to speak to Rowan that way."

"She won't. I will reprimand her later. But for now, let her comfort her daughter."

A hand slipped into mine, and I immediately felt that warm, soothing energy that was Lucas.

"I'm fine. She should be able to speak her mind," I said, trying to keep my voice calm and even.

"No, she shouldn't," Anson said, coming up alongside me

and sliding a hand along the small of my back. "It's disrespect and it can't stand. If it does, others in the pack might think it's okay to target you."

My stomach pitched. "Why would they want to target me?"

Keene sent me a sympathetic look. "Plenty of people want to be at the top. And they might not appreciate the new girl coming in and taking that spot."

CHAPTER FORTY-SIX

"**Y**OU'RE HERE!"
A small form slammed into me, wrapping me in a hug, and I couldn't help the laughter that bubbled out of me. "Crispin, I missed you."

He tilted his head back, smiling widely at me. "I missed you too. Dad said you're going to be here for a while."

I looked up at Sam as he strode into the lodge. "I am. Hi, Sam."

"Hey, Rowan. The little man was over the moon when I told him you were here."

"I'm not little," Crispin growled.

Sam pressed his lips together to keep from grinning. "Big man, sorry."

Crispin slipped his hand into mine. "We're having breakfast with you today, but no one else gets to come."

My gaze met Sam's in question.

He sent me a reassuring smile. "Mason didn't want to overwhelm you right off the bat, and I think there were some things he wanted to talk about."

I fought the groan that wanted to surface. What else was about to throw me for a loop?

"Breakfast is ready," Keene called as he peeked his head out from the dining area. He gave Sam and Crispin a chin lift. "Hey, guys."

We made our way towards what smelled like a delicious feast. My stomach growled. After the scene with Jasmine, I hadn't had much of an appetite yesterday. I'd spent most of the day sketching on the back deck, while Holden holed up with his dad and the rest of the guys worked on homework.

I'd needed to lose myself in pastels on paper, processing the events of the past few days. The guys seemed to sense that, sticking close but giving me the time to disappear into my own head for a while. I didn't find any real answers, but I felt a little less frenetic.

One of the back doors to the lodge opened, and Vaughn appeared. Crispin stepped between me and Vaughn, as if he might protect me. Vaughn's lips twitched. "Morning, Crispin."

"I like Ro, and I don't want you to hurt her."

My heart stuttered in my chest. There was warmth at Crispin's care for me and pain at what Vaughn faced on a daily basis. I stepped around Crispin and moved straight to Vaughn. My arms circled his waist, and I pulled him close in a hug. "Vaughn won't hurt me."

Vaughn froze for a moment, and then his arms slowly came around me. I swore my soul sighed, feeling less strained somehow. Vaughn squeezed my waist. "You can't do that. I might not always be in control."

"I trust you," I whispered.

"You shouldn't."

A throat cleared and Vaughn dropped his arms, stepping away from me. Mason gave us a tight smile. "Please, come eat. We have things to discuss."

My appetite fled at his words. I twisted the tail of my bracelets around my finger, cutting off my circulation.

Vaughn placed a palm on the small of my back. "It'll be okay."

I sucked in a slow breath and nodded, moving forward. The dining area was on the other side of the fireplace. There were at least twenty tables scattered around, and guilt pricked at me that I'd probably ostracized the pack from their normal breakfast tradition.

Keene's gaze zeroed in on me and his brother, and he smiled. "Jase made biscuits and gravy. Ro, they're the best thing you've ever tasted."

Vaughn and I took a seat next to Keene. Sam and Crispin sat on one side of Mason, while Holden and Lucas sat on the other. Anson strode in from the kitchen and set a Diet Coke in front of me, winking.

The simple gesture made my eyes burn. "Thank you."

He bent, giving me a quick kiss. "Gotta take care of my girl." Vaughn let out a soft growl, but Anson just rolled his eyes. "*Our* girl, you know what I mean."

The platter of food was passed around, but Keene served me before I could take it from him. "Trust me, you'll want seconds."

I took a small bite and almost moaned, the flavors were incredible. "This is amazing."

"Told ya," he said.

Mason set his coffee mug down on the table. "Before you head off to school today, I'd like to take a blood sample to run a few tests."

Everyone quieted, and I set my fork down on my plate. "What kind of tests?"

"Most importantly, your lineage. The majority of our packs are in a database, similar to how human DNA testing works."

"Dad, you said you'd give her time," Holden argued.

He sent his son a silencing look. "That time has run out. We need all the information we can get about Rowan. This is to help her. Knowing where she comes from, hopefully speaking with her birth parents, will aid in that."

Holden opened his mouth to argue, but I spoke up. "It's okay. We can do the blood test now."

Delaying it only meant that it would be hanging over my head. Better to get it over with. But the idea of finally knowing who my parents were, why they'd given me up, had my stomach doing a series of acrobatics.

Mason smiled at me, but it didn't quite reach his eyes. "Thank you, Rowan."

The various conversations picked back up again, and Vaughn pushed my plate closer to me. "Eat."

I scowled at him. "Give me a second, would you?"

"I heard your stomach growl, and Keene said you barely ate yesterday."

"When did he tell you that?" I sent a glare in Keene's direction.

"Just now," Vaughn answered. At my perplexed look, Vaughn tapped the side of his head. "All pack members have a mental link. We can speak to the pack as a whole or to specific members. You'll have that link too, once you shift and become an official member."

My jaw fell open. "Why are you guys always keeping the cool stuff from me?"

Vaughn chuckled. "There's plenty more where that came from."

For the first time, a trickle of excitement flowed through me. I was going to turn into a wolf. And who knew what kind of powers I'd have.

Lucas sent me a wink from across the table. "I can't wait to run with you in your wolf form."

A pleasant shiver ran down my spine at his words. "Can I see you in your wolf forms?" I'd seen Holden, Anson, and Vaughn, but not Keene and Lucas. And I wanted a chance to really take them in when we weren't under attack.

Lucas' eyes heated. "After school."

I nodded and took another sip of my Diet Coke. I forced myself to eat more of the delicious meal, even though my stomach was still on a roller-coaster ride. When I finally pushed my plate aside, Sam stood.

"I'll get my kit, and we can take your blood in the living room."

"You know how to do that?" I squeaked.

He smiled at me. "Don't worry, I'm a certified EMT. I've got needles down pat."

"Luc, you sit with her and hold her hand so it doesn't hurt," Anson ordered.

I scowled at him. "You're not forcing Lucas to take my pain while I get blood drawn."

Lucas pushed back from the table and stood. "I want to do it."

I got to my feet but held out a hand to halt him. "No. I can handle a freaking little prick." Then I glanced at Crispin. "You'll hold my hand, right?"

Crispin's chest puffed up. "Of course."

Vaughn chuckled, shaking his head, but the rest of the guys glared at the nine-year-old.

Crispin and I led the way into the living room, sitting down on the sofa. Crispin held my hand tightly. "Don't worry, Dad's good at this."

"Thanks, big man."

I rolled up my sleeve as Sam pulled a few things out of his kit. He wrapped a band around my arm and swiped an alcohol swab over the crook of my elbow. "Just a quick pinch."

I closed my eyes and Crispin squeezed my hand, but I barely felt anything at all. A minute later, Sam pressed a cotton ball to my arm. "All done."

My eyes popped open. "That's it?"

Sam laughed. "Not bad, right?"

"Not bad at all."

But as I looked at the vial of dark red liquid, I couldn't help but wonder if that small container had the ability to turn my life on its head once again.

CHAPTER FORTY-SEVEN

"THINK WE COULD PLAY HOOKY TODAY?" I ASKED AS we pulled into the school parking lot.

We'd forgone two vehicles today and all piled into Anson's Range Rover. I could see heads swiveling towards the SUV as we made our way through the maze of cars.

Anson shot me a devilish look in the rearview mirror. "We could go to my house and…"

Holden smacked him upside the head. "The last thing we need is the school calling Rowan's dad and telling him she's not here."

I hadn't heard a peep from my dad since that one text message. No "how are you?" No "I'm sorry." Nothing.

Anson pulled into his usual parking space. "Fine. Can we go back to my place after school at least?"

Holden shook his head. "My dad wants us back at the compound."

Keene groaned. "Mason lifted the ban on the lodge after breakfast, so you know people are going to be crawling all over the place, wanting a look at Ro."

My stomach gave a healthy flip as I shifted in my seat. Lucas linked his fingers with mine, his warmth pouring into me. "Don't worry, we can hide out in Holden's room if we need to."

"Or go to Vaughn's and my cabin," Keene offered.

"I can't hide forever," I said softly.

Lucas swept his thumb back and forth across my hand. "No, but you don't have to push yourself too much at once." He winced. "But my parents and little sister do want to meet you."

Parents. I'd gotten used to so few of the guys having parental figures around that I'd almost forgotten Lucas had parents. "Of course. Whenever they want." My stomach twisted. What if I wasn't what they wanted for their son? What if they hated the fact that I had four other mates besides him?

Lucas leaned in, nuzzling my neck. "They're going to love you."

"I'd settle for them not hating me."

Holden turned around and faced me. "Luc's parents are the nicest people ever. You won't have any issues with them."

"What about the rest of the pack?" I mumbled.

Anson turned off the vehicle and twisted in his seat. "I'm not exactly Mr. Popular when it comes to the pack. We can be black sheep together."

Holden scowled at Anson. "You're not a black sheep and neither is Rowan."

Anson shrugged. "I'm not exactly welcomed with open arms either. I just want Ro to know she's not alone if she feels a cold shoulder."

I scooted forward, wrapping my hands around Anson's arm and leaning my forehead onto his. "You're not alone either. Never again."

With Anson's cocky confidence, I forgot how isolated he often felt.

Anson inhaled deeply, tipping his face to my neck. "Really fucking wish we weren't in the school parking lot right now."

I couldn't help the laughter that bubbled out of me. I released my hold on Anson's arm and framed his face with my hands, leaning in for a slow kiss.

"Hell," Keene muttered. "It's going to be a long day."

I released my hold on Anson and sat back, pressing my lips to Keene's neck. "You'll make it."

He wrapped an arm around me and dropped a kiss to my head. "Barely."

"Sitting around here isn't going to make it any easier," Holden said, opening his car door.

I sighed and leaned over Keene, opening our door as well. "Let's go."

Keene slid out, then me, and Lucas even followed instead of getting out on his side. I looked back at him, raising a brow in question.

"I want to stick close, just in case," he informed me.

The drama of the last time I was here filled my mind. The ugly posters. Running out of school. No wonder people were staring.

We made our way inside, the guys surrounding me. Any time someone would focus too intensely on me, Anson would snarl at them. I pinched his side. "Quit it. That's just making things worse."

He pulled me closer into his side. "They need to back off."

I slipped my hand under the hem of his T-shirt, pressing my palm into his back. "They will. Eventually, I'll become old news and they'll move on."

Holden sent me a doubtful look. "I hope you're right. But do me a favor? Wait for one of us to walk you between classes, okay?"

Those four sets of eyes focused on me were pleading.

"Oh fine, but we're not doing this forever." I had to hope that once I shifted and we knew who attacked me, they'd relax a little, trusting that I could protect myself.

Holden gave me a quick kiss. "Have a good class."

"You too."

Holden and Keene headed down the hall and the rest of us piled into astronomy. Ridge and Jack were already seated and gave us a wave.

"How are you feeling?" Jack asked.

"Completely back to normal." I glanced at Ridge as I slid into an empty desk, my cheeks heating. "I really appreciate you and Cass going to get my things."

He sent me a smile. "No problem. Your mom's a piece of work. Glad you'll be with us now."

My blush deepened. I could only imagine what Ridge might've overheard when he and Cass were at my house.

"Her mom's smart," Sadie quipped as she and one of her friends moved down the row of desks.

Anson stiffened next to me. "Get lost, Sadie."

She ignored him and stayed focused on me, a smile playing on her lips. "Not even your own parents want you. How sad is that?" She chuckled, but it was an ugly sound. "Wait, this is your second set of parents that don't want you, right? That has to be a record. Give it time, these guys will leave you too. And I can't wait to have a front-row seat."

All the guys around me sent Sadie death glares. Lucas leaned forward, massaging my shoulders. "Don't listen to her."

"I know."

Sadie was angry and deeply unhappy. But I also wondered if there was a kernel of truth in her words.

CHAPTER FORTY-EIGHT

I LEANED INTO LUCAS' SIDE AS HOLDEN CLIMBED INTO THE back seat behind me. I let Lucas' arms wrap around me, that warm energy swirling within me again. I needed every last bit of it. The day had been one of the longest I could remember.

Sadie and her bitch squad had been out in full force, and Jasmine had officially joined their ranks. The snide comments and whispers had peppered me from my first class to my last. A boy I'd never met had come up to me and told me that if I sucked his dick, I could live with him too. Anson had punched him in the face.

Thankfully, no teachers had seen, and Keene had grabbed hold of him at the last second, making the punch less potent. But the guy would still be rocking a black eye. I couldn't find it in myself to feel bad for him.

Holden laced his fingers with mine as Anson started the SUV, and Keene tapped out a text on his phone. "I'm sorry today was so rough."

"It's not your fault."

There was doubt in Holden's expression, and I shifted in my seat so I was facing him. "It's not."

He traced a line on my palm with his thumb. "We could've let you be, then you wouldn't be mixed up in this mess."

My ribs tightened around my lungs, making it difficult to take a full breath. "Don't say that."

"Shit," he muttered, pulling me into his arms. "We're not going anywhere. Don't worry, Ro."

The tension in me eased a fraction, but not enough. Holden rubbed a hand up and down my back as Anson drove. "I'm sorry. I shouldn't have said that. I just hate how fixated people have become on you."

"I can deal with it. What I can't handle is you bailing on me."

Keene twisted in his seat, glaring at Holden. His expression softened as he focused on me. "Never gonna happen. You're stuck with us."

"I like being stuck with you."

"Good," Anson grunted, and I couldn't help but smile.

We were quiet the rest of the drive, all of us lost in our own worlds, trying to process everything that was changing so rapidly. When Anson pulled up in front of the lodge, Mason stepped out with four people in tow. Coby, Sam, and two people I didn't recognize—a man and a woman. The man wrapped his arm around the woman, pulling her into his side.

"Those are my parents," Lucas said softly.

I straightened immediately, looking down at my outfit. Was this appropriate? Had I spilled something on myself at lunch? I could be a clumsy eater.

Lucas pressed a kiss to my temple. "You look beautiful, and I already told you that they're going to love you."

Anson studied the group through his window. "This looks pretty damn official."

Holden straightened. "My dad said he has something to talk to us about."

"I don't know if I can take many more bombs being dropped," I said quietly.

Keene turned, pressing his forehead to mine. "Yes, you can. You're stronger than you know."

A flash of movement caught my attention, and Vaughn stepped out of the woods, striding towards the SUV. "Why do I feel like I'm in trouble?"

"I think it's hard for him to be away from you all day. Makes his wolf edgy," Keene explained.

I motioned for Lucas to let me out. He opened the door and jumped out. I followed but kept moving, going straight for Vaughn. A slight shudder ran through him at my approach. I didn't let the hesitancy in his gaze stop me. I wrapped my arms around his waist and pressed my cheek to his chest.

His arms came around me quicker this time, and I swore I felt him sigh. "Keene said people were mean to you today."

I mentally screamed at Keene. Vaughn would probably come to school as my bodyguard tomorrow, ripping the heads off anyone who looked at me sideways.

"I'm fine."

"You're not. I can feel it."

I tilted my head back so that I could see his face. "You felt it?"

He nodded. "I knew you were hurting somehow." There was confusion in his expression, wariness, but also, a fierce protectiveness. "They need to shield you better."

My hands fisted in Vaughn's T-shirt. "They do, but no one can stop words."

"I could," he grunted.

"But I really don't want you to go on a murderous rampage to stop a few mean girls."

Vaughn's lips twitched. "Noted."

That slightest moment sent a pang of heat to my belly. Vaughn's dark and broody look worked for him big-time. But Vaughn with a hint of a smile? Catastrophic.

Our lips were so close, just a breath away. It would be so easy to close that distance. Everything in me was crying out for more from Vaughn.

Heat flashed in those ice-blue eyes. Then, without warning, he released me and stepped back.

I tried not to take it personally. I knew that there were more than a few demons making a home inside Vaughn's head, but that didn't change the fact that his retreat killed something in me.

"Rowan," Mason called from the steps. "We need to talk."

"Great," I muttered under my breath.

I started towards the lodge, Vaughn at my back and the rest of the guys moving in to flank me.

Lucas' mom sent me a smile. It looked as if she wanted it to be reassuring, but the movement wavered, as if she couldn't quite hold it. "I'm Lara. It's so lovely to meet you." I took the hand she extended. Lara didn't shake my hand but took it and held it between hers. "You're a blessing to us. I'm so glad Luc found you."

My eyes and throat burned. "Thank you. It's wonderful to meet you."

"I'm sure a little overwhelming too," Lucas' dad said as he stepped forward. "I'm Greg. We promise not to crowd you too much. This is quite the adjustment period for you."

I couldn't help the soft laugh that escaped. "It's definitely that."

He patted my shoulder. "You'll get there. Don't you fret."

The guys had been right. There was nothing to fear with Lara and Greg. The only thing I felt wafting off of them was kindness and warmth, with maybe a little worry mixed in.

"Let's go inside," Mason suggested.

"Could you just tell me right here?" I asked. I didn't want to bring this inside. I just wanted it over with, whatever it was he had to drop on me.

Coby stepped forward, her eyes narrowing on me. "We'll have this conversation where the alpha wants."

Mason held up a hand to silence her. "Everyone in this pack is free to speak their minds, as long as it's done respectfully." He turned to me. "Ripping off the bandage?"

"It's better than doing it slowly."

Holden pushed in on one side of me, Lucas on the other, and I could feel Vaughn's heat at my back. Something inside me could sense that Anson and Keene were here too.

"We know who your mother is."

Mason said the words calmly and evenly, but I could feel the tension running through the others around us.

"There's more," I said. Not a question, but a statement of fact.

"She was a member of this pack."

"What?" Holden barked.

Tears filled Lara's eyes. "Now that I know, I can see the resemblance. Similar hair and eyes to Abigail."

"Y-you know her?"

She stepped forward. "We were best friends."

I noticed the use of past tense in her statement. "Where is she?"

"We don't know. Your mother went missing eighteen years ago. No one's seen her since."

CHAPTER FORTY-NINE

THE WORLD AROUND ME FLICKERED IN AND OUT. THERE was a buzzing in my ears as someone guided me up the steps and into the lodge. I was settled between Holden and Anson, Keene and Lucas flanking them. And I could feel Vaughn's energy prowling back and forth behind the couch.

"What do you mean *missing?*"

Mason sank down on the couch opposite us, Sam and Coby on either side, while Lara and Greg took chairs in between us. "Eighteen years ago, Abigail went to Seattle. She said she wanted to go see an art exhibit. She planned on staying the night and returning the next day. I felt her link with the pack sever hours after she left."

"D-does that mean she's dead?" I couldn't keep my voice from trembling as I spoke.

Holden squeezed my hand, hard. "No. A death feels different."

"Anyone can sever the pack link at any time," Mason explained.

"Or that sever can be forced," Anson added.

Lucas scowled at him. "Not helpful."

I held up a hand to stop the arguing before it began. "No.

I need to know the full picture." I met Luc's gaze. "Don't keep things from me in the hopes of protecting me."

His jaw worked back and forth. "All right."

I turned back to Mason, silently encouraging him to continue.

"I sent enforcers there immediately to investigate."

My eyes shifted to Sam in question. He nodded. "I wasn't head enforcer then, but I was with the group who went. We found her car near the gallery and followed her scent inside. Then it was like she just vanished."

"She must've been pregnant with me, right?"

Mason shifted in his seat. "We can usually scent when a female is pregnant, but there are ways to disguise it if the female wants to keep the news private for a time."

"My father?" I croaked. "Do you know who that is?"

Coby scoffed. "Who knows. She could've been sleeping with anyone."

Mason let out a low growl, and Coby's head lowered.

Lara turned to me. "I knew she was seeing someone, but she wouldn't tell me who. He wasn't in our pack. But she told me she'd ended things with him about a month before she went missing."

My stomach cramped, and my grip on Holden's hand tightened. "He couldn't have hurt her, right? I mean, I'm here. She gave birth at some point."

Coby rolled her eyes. "You guys are glossing over the easiest explanation. Abigail probably slept with someone she shouldn't have, a mated male. She likely ran to hide that fact."

Lara sprang to her feet. "Shut up! You barely knew Abbie, and you were always competitive with her because of her gift."

"Gift?"

Mason's mouth curved into the slightest of smiles. "She was

one of the most attuned empaths I've ever encountered and a great gift to our pack."

Lucas straightened. "I remember Mom talking about her."

Lara's expression softened as she looked at her son. "I so wish she could've mentored you. I think you two would've been two peas in a pod."

My heart clenched, that pang of missing someone I didn't even know striking deep. "And no one's heard from her since?"

Lara shook her head. "Not a word."

"I have some contacts I can reach out to," Mason said. "We'll start the search again. We could get lucky."

But what were the chances we'd find a woman who had hidden herself for almost two decades? If she was even still alive to be found.

———⊰❋⊱———

I leaned against the rock, balancing the sketch pad in my lap. I focused on my strokes against the page, wondering if it was my mother who had given me my love of art. She'd enjoyed it enough to make the trek to Seattle to see an exhibit.

My pencil slipped, sending a black line across the paper. I fought the urge to growl. There was no way to erase it without taking intricate pieces of the drawing with it.

I stared out at the lake. It was away from the lodge and other populated areas, but still firmly in the heart of the compound. This was as alone as I was going to get. But I needed even this illusion of solitude.

I couldn't take much more of the guys' pitying looks and the whispers as I'd pass other people in the pack—everyone wondering why Abigail had given me up.

I closed the sketchbook and hugged it to my chest. As if that could somehow give me comfort. There was a tugging sensation in my chest, and I knew my time was running out. It wasn't just my body telling me I needed to seek out my bond, it was my heart too. Only an hour or so away from them and I missed their comforting presence.

I shoved my belongings into my bag and climbed to my feet. A rustling sounded in the woods and I paused, straining to listen. There was nothing.

I slid my bag over my shoulder and started down the path towards the lodge and the center of the compound. The sun was low in the sky, and I knew I needed to hustle to make the walk back before it got dark.

I picked up my pace, stepping over tree roots and around rocks. Maybe this would be my new place. It wasn't as peaceful as the raging creek, but that was outside the compound bounds. This lake would have to be it for now.

Voices caught on the air and my footsteps slowed.

"Holden, please. Look at me. You know it's good between us. I'm what you need. Rowan is too weak to lead this pack. It's not her fault, but that doesn't change the truth." Jasmine's voice took on a tone I'd never heard from her before, soft, almost submissive.

"You have to stop. This is going to happen, Jaz. Rowan is my *mate*. You know everything changes when a wolf finds that."

I stepped forward as quietly as possible, knowing that their shifter hearing would pick up on any little sound. The path curved in front of me, and I stepped behind a tree, peeking to the side of it. Jasmine stood close to Holden, almost touching, and I had to swallow back a growl.

"You don't have to accept the mate bond," Jaz urged. "We have free will for a reason. You need to make the hard choice for the good of the pack. For the good of us." She rested a hand on his chest, over his heart. "I haven't forgotten that night. I know you felt it too."

Air whooshed out of my lungs as she pushed in even closer to Holden. He laid a hand over hers. "That kiss was a mistake, Jaz. It never should've happened. I'm sorry if that hurts you, but it's the truth."

Pain shot along my sternum. *That kiss.* I thought of all the times Holden had sworn to me there had never been anything but friendship between him and Jasmine. How easily the lies had slipped from his tongue.

She closed the distance. I watched as if it were happening in slow motion, her lips meeting his. He was pushing her away but not before I let out a pained sound. It was so soft, I barely heard it myself, but Holden's head whipped in my direction. "Rowan—"

"No." My voice didn't shake even though the rest of me trembled. "Stay away from me."

There was no excuse or pretty lie that would be good enough. I couldn't even bear to look at him. So I took my only option. I turned and fled.

CHAPTER FIFTY

BRANCHES SLAPPED MY FACE AS I RAN THROUGH THE woods. It was dumb, completely idiotic, running with no idea of where I was going. All I knew was that I needed to get away. From the secrets and lies. From one life-altering bomb after another.

I dodged trees as best I could, my lungs burning. I caught sight of the pond again, but at a different angle than where I had been before. Just as I was about to break through the trees, I slammed into someone.

Hands came to my shoulders, steadying me. "Whoa there."

Sam's concerned face came into focus in my vision. "Sorry, I…" My words trailed off. I had no idea how to finish that sentence.

"No apology needed. Are you okay?"

I bit my bottom lip to keep from crying. "No." It was the only word I could muster. I was as far from okay as humanly possible.

He pulled me into a hug, awkwardly patting my back. "It'll be all right. I know this is a lot right now."

I nodded against his shoulder, my throat burning. It wouldn't be all right. Not when I couldn't trust one of my bond to tell me the truth. When another member of that bond didn't even want me to touch him.

I pulled out of Sam's hold, wiping at my face where scratches stung. "I'll be fine. I really am sorry I ran into you. I wasn't looking where I was going."

Sam chuckled. "You hit like a linebacker."

I tried to smile, but I couldn't seem to get my lips to obey. The image of Jasmine's mouth on Holden's playing on a loop in my mind. My stomach pitched, and I closed my eyes, inhaling through my nose.

Sam's hand went to my shoulder. "Why don't we get you back to the lodge. You came quite a ways off the beaten path."

I looked around me and realized I didn't have the first clue how to get back, even if it was the last place I wanted to go. "Thanks. I'd appreciate that."

"Follow me." Sam started through the trees, picking an unseen path that was wide enough for us to walk side by side. "Mason put me on the task force to look for your mom, for Abigail."

"That's good." My pulse thrummed in my temples. I didn't have brain space for missing mothers right now, not when all I could see was Jasmine and Holden.

"Do you have any memory of her?"

I shook my head. "My parents adopted me when I was only a month old. But it was a closed adoption, so they didn't even know my mother's name. All they had were a few details about her health history." Missing one tiny detail. That there was a chance I'd turn into a wolf.

Sam made a humming noise as he kept walking. "And they don't know where you were born?"

"No. The adoption agency was in Baltimore, but they took placements from all over the country."

"I'll have to get the name from you so I can see about breaking into their records."

My steps faltered. "You can do that?"

Sam chuckled. "In my sleep. Keene too. He's even better than me."

"Whoa."

I started walking again, looking around me. "I could've sworn the lodge was the other way. My sense of direction is the worst."

Sam's smile was tight. "We have to go down a bit to get to a bridge to cross the stream."

A prickle of unease slid through me. "Oh."

We were quiet for a bit as we walked, the sun dropping even lower in the sky. The only sounds I heard were the distant flow of water and the wind in the trees. I shivered as the breeze picked up.

Sam caught the movement out of the corner of his eye. "You won't have to worry about ever being cold soon."

"I won't?"

"Wolf shifters run hot. It's also almost impossible for us to catch human illnesses."

"No cancer or anything like that?" I glanced over my shoulder in the direction that I thought the lodge was. We were moving farther and farther away. I needed that damn telepathic walkie-talkie system the other guys had.

"Nope. We have other risks, but not that."

"It's too bad we don't know what protects us from those diseases. We could help a lot of people."

Sam shot a look in my direction. "It would leave us too exposed. We'd all end up as lab rats."

I looked over my shoulder again. "I feel like we're getting farther away."

"It's the long way around. But it gives me time to talk to you."

My steps slowed until I stopped altogether. "About what?"

Sam turned to face me. "I know who your father is."

CHAPTER FIFTY-ONE

"WHAT?" THE SINGLE WORD CAME OUT ON A whoosh of air.

"I know who your father is, and he wants to help you."

I took an instinctive step back. Help me. What did that mean? "Who is he?"

Sam took a slow step forward. "We'll tell you everything once I get you to him. You aren't safe here."

My heart picked up its pace as I took another step back. "Why can't he come here?"

A hulking figure stepped out of the trees. "Yes, Sam. Why can't he come here?" Vaughn's ice-blue eyes flashed in the low light as he stalked towards us.

Sam's head whipped in Vaughn's direction, a snarl on his lips. "Don't concern yourself with this, *pup*."

Vaughn prowled forward, stepping between me and Sam. "I'm no pup. Haven't been one since I was eleven and lived through hell on earth."

My heart stuttered at his words, pain slicing through me.

"The pack is on its way," Vaughn said matter-of-factly. "You can explain why you've been keeping secrets from the alpha."

Sam let a slew of curses fly. "Rowan, this is your choice. You can come with me."

I shook my head. As much of a mess as my life was, I was willing to fight for the guys in my bond. "No."

Anger lit in Sam's eyes. "I didn't want it to come to this." He let out a low whistle, and two brown wolves appeared from the trees behind Sam.

Vaughn tensed, his hands fisting at his sides. "This is suicide, Sam. Run now, and you might make it."

Sam's lip curled. "It'll take them at least twenty minutes to get here, and that's at a dead run. Plenty of time to kill you."

"Stop. I'll go with you." The words were out of my mouth before I could stop them. The image of someone hurting Vaughn, or worse, was more than I could live with.

"No," Vaughn snarled. His chest heaved as he glared at Sam. "Have you forgotten my gift so easily?"

A hint of wariness filled Sam's expression. "You can only use it in human form. My friends here will rip you to pieces before you have a chance."

Vaughn moved in a flash, his palm landing square on Sam's chest. The effect was instantaneous, as if Sam had been hit with an electric force. His body convulsed in a series of seizures. He crumpled to the ground, his mouth open in a silent scream.

The wolves didn't hesitate, both of them launching at Vaughn.

"Run!" he yelled, just before he shifted into his glorious black wolf form.

One of the brown wolves sank his teeth into Vaughn's flank, while the other charged him, sending him to the ground. I glanced frantically around, looking for any sort of weapon. My gaze settled on a rock the size of a softball, and I ran to pick it up.

A snarl sounded as Vaughn's claws raked across one of the wolves' chests. I didn't wait. I hurled the rock at the wolf. My aim rang true, hitting him in the flank. It startled him enough to lose focus. Vaughn's teeth sank into the wolf's neck, and he sent him flying into a tree.

The action gave the other brown wolf an opening. He launched himself at Vaughn, his teeth sinking into Vaughn's side. Vaughn let out a howl that had my skin prickling and a sharp pain lancing through my chest.

No. No. No. This wasn't happening.

Vaughn struggled to right himself as the other wolf tore at his stomach. Sam moaned on the ground. I searched frantically for any other rock or stick large enough to do damage.

Vaughn let out another howl, and it was as if something deep inside me flared to life. There was a burn and then a flash of light. Pain, as if all my bones were breaking, seared through me. I stumbled, blinking as I sucked in breath. Only I wasn't on two feet, I was on four.

I took in the reddish fur of my paws for a moment before another howl from Vaughn had me snapping into action. Instinct took over, and I charged the brown wolf, jaws snapping. My teeth ripped at his side, taking him by surprise.

He growled low at me, motioning with his head. Did he seriously think I would follow him? I let out my own growl standing between him and Vaughn, who lay panting on the ground, barely moving.

The brown wolf dashed forward, nipping my front leg. I didn't hesitate going right for his neck. The taste of blood on my tongue made my stomach roil, but I ignored it.

The brown wolf snarled, his claws raking across my stomach.

Pain bloomed bright, but I dove for him again. I had to hold him off.

He bit into my hind leg, and I cried out. But as I did, a series of howls sounded in the forest. Close. I could feel them, my bond. They were so close.

The brown wolf's head snapped up at the sound. He looked at Sam, still writhing on the ground, and then took off from the direction he came.

Four wolves charged into the clearing. I knew they were mine immediately, even Lucas and Keene, who I hadn't seen in wolf form before. But my gaze immediately flew back to Vaughn. I rushed over to him, nosing him with my snout.

He didn't react. I watched his chest rise and fall, but his breathing was far too shallow. Then it stopped altogether.

CHAPTER FIFTY-TWO

I SHIFTED BACK WITHOUT EVEN THINKING ABOUT IT. My muscles strained and bones popped. Then I was on two legs again. They shook as I fell to my knees, not caring in the least that I was as naked as the day I was born, my clothes lost somewhere in my shift.

"Vaughn." His name was a harsh whisper on my lips.

"Rowan! You're bleeding." Lucas was at my side in a flash, his hand going to my stomach.

I could hear Anson and Holden in my mind now. They were running after the brown wolf. I could hear Mason too, telling them he was following. Other wolves filled the clearing, ones I didn't recognize.

Keene rushed over to us. His silver gray coat had a black patch on the chest. It was that same almost heart-shape that Vaughn had, but in reverse. His shape blurred, and then he was human again. "Vaughn." He pressed his face into his brother's neck and something in me broke.

Tears poured from my eyes, and I shook Lucas off of me. "Give me space."

"Ro, you can't heal this. He's too far gone," Lucas said quietly.

"I have to try." My voice broke on the words, but my hands reached out, sinking into Vaughn's fur. There was something there. A life force of sorts. And I knew Vaughn wasn't gone. Not yet.

"He's still alive." I focused on my hands, the same feeling from when I'd healed Anson's cut. I tried to grab hold of that hum of energy within me, the spark I'd felt when I first touched Vaughn. Then I pushed it into him with everything I had in me.

My heart stuttered, skipping a few beats, and Lucas steadied me with his hands.

His fingers tightened on my shoulders. "You can't do this. It's taking too much. I can feel it."

Keene's eyes flew from his brother to me. There was a look of such desperation on him. He didn't know what to ask of me. To give up? To keep pushing?

"Keene, say something," Lucas ordered.

"I-I can't. I…" His words trailed off, not able to finish his sentence.

Lara rushed over to us. "She needs you. All of you."

She must have told Anson and Holden the same through the pack link because I heard whispers in my head that they were coming.

I pushed more energy into Vaughn, wavering on my knees. Keene hurried to my side, placing his hands on my waist, helping to steady me. I felt a small burst of something flow through me, and I pushed it all into Vaughn.

A slow rhythmic thumping grew louder. I knew it was Vaughn. His heart was coming back. It was working. But as I stared at the blood seeping from his gut wound, I knew it wasn't enough.

I pushed harder, my vision going blurry.

Hurry! Lara called through the mind link.

Holden and Anson bounded into the clearing, shifting

mid-stride. They ran to my side, dropping to their knees and immediately placing hands on me. Anson gripped my thigh, while Holden's hands went to my back.

There was another surge. Light flashed behind my eyes, and I focused everything into Vaughn. "Don't leave us," I whispered in a half-plea, half-prayer.

A burning pain seared the front of my hip as if someone had pressed a branding iron into me.

"The bond," Holden gritted out through clenched teeth. "It's starting."

I breathed through the pain, keeping my eyes closed and guiding all that light into Vaughn. I let my head fall forward onto his side, unable to keep upright anymore.

"This is too much," Lucas said. "I can feel her fading."

"Then we need to feed her more energy," Anson growled.

"Holy shit," said a voice I didn't recognize. "His flesh is knitting back together."

My eyes fluttered open, my head still resting on Vaughn's fur. His coat was stitching itself back together as if by magic. The sight gave me all I needed for one last push. I reached as deep as I could, imagining a reservoir of golden light that went down to my toes. I pulled as hard as possible and then shoved that light into Vaughn.

An explosion sounded overhead. Sparks danced in my vision. My heart seized in my chest. Then there was nothing but black.

THE END...FOR NOW...

Rowan's story continues in Mark of Stars,
book two in the Shifting Fate *series.*

ACKNOWLEDGMENTS

I have been a reverse harem fan for years. Ideas for some of my own stories have been swirling in my mind for nearly as long. But this was finally the year I put pen to paper and created Rowan and her mates. I hope you've fallen in love with them as I have.

So many people have walked with me on this journey. A huge thank you to my editorial team, proofers, and cover designers. To the couple of early readers of this book who gave me such enthusiastic encouragement. And to my amazing writer friends who have cheered me on every step of the way.

But most of all, thank YOU! Yes, you, the reader of these pages. I'm so grateful you picked up this book.

ALSO BY TESSA HALE

The Shifting Fate Series

Spark of Fate

Mark of Stars

Bond of Destiny

CONNECT WITH TESSA

You can find Tessa at various places on the internet.
These are her favorites...

Website
www.tessahale.com

Newsletter
www.tessahale.com/newsletter

Facebook Page
bit.ly/TessaHaleFB

Facebook Reader Group
bit.ly/TessaHaleBookHangout

Instagram
www.instagram.com/tessahalewrites

Goodreads
bit.ly/TessaHaleGR

BookBub
www.bookbub.com/authors/tessa-hale

Amazon
bit.ly/TessaHaleAmazon

ABOUT TESSA HALE

Author of love stories with magic, usually with more than one
love interest. Constant daydreamer.

Printed in Great Britain
by Amazon